CAPE COD CASKET

CAPE
COD
CASKET

Lockhart Amerman

Harcourt, Brace & World, Inc., New York

None of the characters in this book represents,
save by sheerest coincidence, any existing person.

For Tabby

τοῦ ποιῆσαι βιβλία πολλὰ
οὐκ ἔστι περασμὸς, καὶ
μελέτη πολλὴ κόπωσις σαρκός.

—*Ecclesiastes* 12:12.

Acknowledgment for guidance both by precept and example is thankfully tendered to Mary Robb (at one time, apparently, a Cape Cod police chief), my secretaries, and as usual Agent 3.1416.

Chapter

1

It was not until I climbed into the seat by the driver that I realized the car was a hearse.

The parking lot at the airfield was dark, its facilities primitive, and its nighttime pierced by no more than the necessary beacons.

The man had met me at the plane itself. "Mr. Flower?" His voice was Down-East. "You the Mr. Flower's to go to Sexton's Prim? Gotcher grips there? Just the one? This way then."

He made no offer to take my bag, and I followed him through the small knot of people quitting or greeting the plane. As we walked, he kept talking to me over his shoulder, leaving remarks behind him like scraps in a paper chase.

"We're in the corner of the field. 'Tisn't far." Unexpectedly, he laughed. "Didn't want nobody to get wrong ideas. Hee-hee. Might as well keep the grip with you. Plenty of room up front."

He held open a massive door; a quiet front-seat light gleamed on the dashboard. As I stowed my bag behind my legs, my glance was caught by a shiny knob alongside an ash tray. It was identified by a little sign—black letters on a rectangle of white. "SAND," it said, "FOR OFFICIATING PRIEST." I remembered vaguely that some clergymen sprinkle grains of earth on the grave.

The big engine purred agreeably, and we bumped across the parking area and turned onto a lighted highway. A quick look at my friend showed his round face smiling as he hunched himself over the wheel. We were in the cab of a big Cadillac, a curtained pane of glass behind us.

"Yessir," said the chauffeur. "Yessir. You're right inside one —one of just what you're thinkin'. Ever ride in one before?"

Startled though I was, I had no wish to appear underprivileged.

"Not often," I said.

"Not often"—he echoed me. "That's a good answer—not often. I like that for an answer. Hee-hee."

The man's rather senseless joviality was getting on my nerves.

"Do you drive this—er—regularly?" I asked him. "I mean —to pick up people at stations and airports and that sort of thing?"

He was convulsed. "To pick up people? Hee-hee. That's about it, now; that's about it."

Silence fell for a mile of darkness. We had left the airport lighting far behind and were moving along briskly between rows of set-out pines. "Keep the Cape green," I remembered. Peculiar vehicle or no, it was good to be back; and as we drove, the wonderful smell of sea and sand sprayed us like a giant atomizer in the hands of a kindly dentist.

We joined Route 6 and the company of numerous slow-moving cars. Cape traffic seems always to run in caravans.

"My name's Vickers." The driver's voice shook with a remnant of laughter. "Charlie Vickers. Been drivin' for Dr. Sarkuss near two years now. You're the one's takin' on the twins—tutorin' 'em, are you?"

"I'm taking on the twins," I said. "I'm not sure how much

they'll learn, though." (The modest note seemed appropriate.) "Tell me, Mr. Vickers, are you a—a mortician?"

"Mortician? Hee-hee!" Mr. Vickers was off again. "Me an undertaker? No, sir! Not Charlie Vickers. I just drive for Dr. Sarkuss—that's all."

I knew very little about my new employment and ventured further. "Do you mean that Dr. Sarx is interested in—in—?"

"Greatest in the world, I'm told, son. Greatest in the world. 'Nobody near him for range and appeal'—heard a fellow say that up at Oyster Harbors other day. Never touches a corpus himself, of course. Not for years, they tell me. Hee-hee."

A curious sense of unreality had been growing over me during the past few minutes. Now I found it difficult to frame a picture—of undertaking at long range. "Oh?" I said cautiously. "I gather he's done rather well at it." The sum Dr. Sarx was willing to pay me for glorified baby-sitting did not suggest that he was feeling the pinch.

"Well? Well, indeed! That man's done very well. And never goes near it. Stays here all year round. Just pulls the wires—hee-hee—just pulls the wires, they say."

I thought the figure in dubious taste. "Then why the hearse?" I asked.

Without an answer, he swung the big car off Route 6, and we began to rumble over a rough dirt road.

"Now I can let her out," he said—and did so. Scrub pine on each side of us alternated with low, thick undergrowth. Here and there a light gleamed in the distance. Now and then through an opening, it was possible to look far into the night and imagine the invisible sea.

We drove through a minimal hamlet and chased another mile of lonely curves. I remember that we had just bounced across an arch-backed culvert when a bang exploded from our left front wheel, the tire hissed, and by Charlie's considerable —if unexpected—skill we lurched and stumbled to a stop.

9

Our lights clicked off, and Mr. Vickers' voice came through the darkness.

"That weren't no blowout, son. Hee-hee."

Now that he mentioned it, I realized that the bang had sounded rather like gunfire.

Chapter

2

I have referred to the fact that I knew very little about my forthcoming job. I had simply replied to an advertisement and been promptly accepted: "Mature teen-ager"—how I loathe that term!—"wanted to tend, amuse eleven-year twins July and August. Adequate leisure, well-staffed country house, handsome wage, foreign language desirable. Apply C. Sarx, Sexton's Prim, West Orleans, Mass. Send photograph and description family circumstances."

I hadn't been too sure what that last phrase meant, but with my father's encouragement, I applied and in due course was notified of acceptance. My plane ticket from Philadelphia to Boston was enclosed—with a down-run flight to the Cape. Some kindly soul had thought to suggest that I bring a tennis racket. And the handsome wage was, if they really paid it, gratifying.

As it happened, my father was on the verge of an Australian junket. He is tied up with the State Department in some way, and the job makes him disappear periodically from my horizon. This time we had managed two weeks together in the Adirondacks after school, a visit that was better than average for us. It looked as if the Cape Cod offer was a good interim-filler for his only son.

"Somewhere or other," he said, "I've heard of this Sarx fellow. It's certainly not a common name. I wonder—not that it makes much difference." But his wonder led him to make one or two discreet inquiries. Of these I was not told the result.

"That chap Sarx," he said, "sounds very interesting." But he wouldn't say anything more.

Neither of us, I feel certain, had any thoughts of hearses or shots in the night.

"Don't open the door," Vickers told me. I had reached for the handle automatically. "We'll fix things from in here. No tellin' what kind of crazy Ayrab's out there in the woods. Take this, if you know how to use it." He pressed into my hands a cold and heavy object. It fitted my fingers like a .45.

"Can you shoot one?"

"Yes," I said. (Side arms have always been a kind of hobby of mine.)

"Then shoot if they make a light. Fire at their fire. But stay down low. Hee-hee."

I was glad he thought it funny and scrunched myself down in the seat. There was nothing to do but stare out the window at the inky wayside.

"They don't know about this," the driver said. Immediately there was a click from our foreparts, followed by a grinding noise. The corner of the car where I was sitting began to rise in a series of humping movements exactly as if someone had been shouldering the punctured tire. No light or movement came from the woods outside.

There was another series of sounds, and I could tell that my companion's corner was rising, too. Some mechanical device or other snapped into place, a small red light showed on the dashboard, and we began to move forward through the dark slowly and bumpily but with remarkably efficient progress.

"Retractable treads?" I whispered.

12

"Yep. Front and rear if we needed 'em. Mighty handy on a cemetery hillside, so the reg'lar driver tells me. Specially in winter, I betcha. Ever been in a graveyard in wintertime?" he asked.

Before I could answer, a shot slammed from behind us to the right, but I was too late to see the flash.

"Hit a tree," said Charles. "Hee-hee. Guess he knows we're movin'. Crazy native!"

I fervently hoped that the native referred to was not typical. I also wondered how long my laughing Jehu planned to drive without lights.

"How can you see?" I wanted to know.

"Been here before, son." He was making a good fifteen miles an hour now, and I vastly admired his ability to keep on a wholly invisible track. Intermittently, he looked to right and left, and I gathered he was steering by landmarks. All at once the crowding pine trees fell away; the sky, which it was possible again to see, appeared a paler blue. Ahead of us lay a considerable space of open field.

The big car wobbled to a stop.

"Just stay by the rear end a minute, will you, son?" He spoke as if nothing unusual had happened. "Don't believe you'll have to use that thing, but if you see anybody coming, pop away. Safety's off." (This latter fact I knew and didn't much care for.) "I've got to make a phone call."

His bulky form moved off into the dark ahead of us, and I stationed myself by the tail gate of the hearse, the pistol heavy in my hand.

There was nothing to see, and the only sound was the occasional crack of twigs, diminishing with Charlie's progress. I must confess that I began to long for someone's cozy fireside—no one's in particular, you understand—just something to stand for a safety symbol.

"O.K. Let's go." Charlie's return had been achieved in silence. In the car he switched the lights on—by which I hoped he meant that there was nothing more to fear. A moment later we passed through an open gate in a low stone wall, and the track along which we had been joggling changed to a well-kept blacktop drive. Against its smoother surface, our caterpillar treads made a curious shuffling sound, like a man walking in slippers much too big for him.

I should be giving you a very wrong impression of my make-up if I suggested that the foregoing events had left me unmoved. I have enjoyed my share of scrapes—and one or two trips with my father that turned into major adventures—but I am by no means Flower the Imperturbable.

I managed no more than a silly protest. "Is this—usual? This shooting business?"

Charlie merely tittered—an odd way, I thought, to demonstrate the well-known New England reticence.

We circled in front of a house, and I was cheered to see that it was a house indeed, big, largely lightless, low-spreading—but not, *par exemple,* a crematorium. No doubt there are many of my age who take the trappings of mortality in stride, but I am not yet one of them. What I had so far gathered as to vehicles, employers, and neighborhood friendliness failed somehow to promise a summer's idyll; I felt that I deserved a little soothing.

"I presume we'll call the police when we get inside?" I ventured the question, but Charlie was unenthusiastic.

"Police? Police is in bed, got any sense. Where them boys?" He gave a faint toot on the horn. It had a low and funerary tone. "Here we are," said Charlie.

He was referring to the appearance of two men, dark of face and solemn of manner. Through outflung double doors they came to us—across a wide porch and down a series of steps. I took them to be house servants of a sort, up late and dressed, it seemed, for cleaning: the light that splashed from the house in their wake revealed them each in a white shirt with the sleeves rolled up, dark trousers, and a dull blue denim apron.

Side by side, they halted at the back door of the hearse—Tweedledum and Tweedledee reporting for duty.

"Got him," said Charlie Vickers, and for a moment I thought that he was talking about me. But the two dark ones nodded at him in approval and, with no further orders, proceeded to unlock the tail gate of the vehicle. With no great appearance of effort, they rolled out from the dark interior a handsome metal casket. Its bronzed top shone in the light thrown from the porch.

It had never occurred to me that we were traveling with cargo—that the body of the hearse was occupied! ("Body of the hearse"—I said the words over to myself with a kind of grim relish.)

But as far as the other participants in the scene were concerned, we were involved in nothing more than routine procedure. With a hand from Charlie, the casket was carried up the steps and into the house, Jonathan Flower bringing up the rear as solitary mourner.

Charlie waved toward a comfortable-looking living room. "I'll take the rocket now," he said. He stretched out his hand, and I gladly surrendered the pistol, a nerve-racking weight in my raincoat pocket.

The chauffeur looked at me coyly. "See here," he said. "Hee-hee-hee." He broke the gun, freed the clip, and ejected the chamber shell. "See? All blanks."

I checked them, and they were.

"Wait here," said Charlie. "I'll just be a couple of minutes. Looks like everybody's gone to bed. I'll be back and show you your room." Whereupon he retreated with the casket and its two attendants down the depths of a hall that led toward the back of the house. It was a wide hall; indeed, the house gave an instant effect of spaciousness. Doors opened left and right off the corridor, and a broad stairway marched above. Oak woodwork, dark-stained floors, and Oriental rugs achieved an atmosphere of somber luxury. In the room where he had left me, a substantial fireplace nursed dying embers. These were of coal, not wood ash, and their glow was broken by the intricacies of a metal screen.

Under brown shades, dim lamps shone on the surface of two tables; but the room was so big that its walls and corners lost themselves in shadow. On one table *Jack and Jill* lay open, rather improbably juxtaposed to *Zeitschrift für Archaeologie*. A pair of murderous-looking chisels lay on the floor. They seemed to me an odd adornment for so dignified a chamber. And the whole apartment was pervaded with the scent of Turkish tobacco.

"You can get breakfast any time from eight to nine-thirty." Charlie was back, dusting his hands against each other with a gesture of mild distaste. "Dr. Sarkuss, sometimes he eats early; sometimes he eats late. Sometimes he don't eat at all. Hee-hee. That's the kind of fellow he is, I guess. Well"—he sounded weary—"you better come along now. You're upstairs over the garage. Kids up there, too, the twins is. Don't forget your grip."

"Look here," I said, gathering up such strength as remained. "I'd really like some sort of explanation. What sort of place is this, anyway? What was the shooting about? And the casket—who's dead?"

"Hee-hee." Charlie laughed. "Ain't nobody dead." (He didn't actually say "ain't," but I shan't attempt to reproduce the flatness of his down-East "a.") "Just a matter of business," he added. "Come along now. You'll meet 'em all in the morning."

I glanced at my watch. It was nearly twelve.

Chapter

3

Charlie Vickers tittered his way with me up a short straight stair—not the ample one I had seen in the hall but an almost ladder-like affair that we gained by a lengthy walk through the first-floor quarters. At its top we threaded a long, straight corridor and arrived at a gray garret. It was a reconstructed loft, apparently, its pegged deck-planking gray as the Minch in December, its low walls papered gray but the woodwork white. An iron bed stared at an ancient Morris chair. The single window was high and open, and a cool, salty breeze fluttered the simple curtains.

But I couldn't get to sleep. All the noises that infect a stillness took their turns. Frogs vocalized. Katydids katied. Then there would be silence till the boards—it seemed of my own flooring—creaked. Then silence. Then the lonely whistle of a distant freight. Under ordinary circumstances, the combination would probably have lulled me. But not at Sexton's Prim.

I decided to read and remembered I had only a Bible. My father had thrust it on me the day before, after commenting on what he called my "addiction to illiterate disintegrates." (By "disintegrates" he means not just the dirty boys but the we've-had-it school.) I can hear him declaiming: "These chaps

have one great asset—they believe in sin, original and otherwise. That much makes sense. They've a healthy awareness of
widespread evil, but because they have never sold themselves
standards, they're not sure whether this sin stuff is pathetic,
angry-making, or lovable. They produce no heroes because
they aren't sure what heroes are made of. Their morality depends on what they've had for lunch, and they write as a rule
from the heart of the bathroom." (This is his usual line. I
haven't bothered to tell him that my own generation has a
very clear idea of the predicament in which *his* finds itself.)

"There's no such hesitancy in the Bible," he had said. "The
villains aren't all black and the heroes don't wear halos; but
by the time you're through, at least you know who's which.
And all along, there's good old God up there, a great and grim
Reality. Your current 'realists' could do with a dose of Him.
Didn't you start to read the Bible through?"

I admitted that I had bogged down in First Samuel.

"Pick it up again then. My word, you're at a high spot—old
Saul crashing about with a split personality and David Robin-
Hooding it. They were men of blood, yes—not of formal-
dehyde." In my present circumstances, I remembered his
words vividly: "Give old Saul another fling!"

So I fished out the thin-leaved Bible and took up where I
had left off, the small bulb hanging by its wire above me
swaying now and then to shift the corner shadows.

Saul was in an evil mood. What with the badgerings of
outlaw David and suspicious behavior on the part of his own
family, he longed for the advice of Samuel, a kind of ecclesias-
tical wise old owl. But the owl was dead, and Saul decided to
consult a medium. Here the text grows delightfully ghastly
because Saul is in disguise and the medium is a witch, and you
can fairly hear the cauldron bubble. (Saul's psychosis doesn't
help matters, either.)

*"And Saul said, I pray thee, divine unto me by the fa-
miliar spirit. . . . and bring me up Samuel.*

And when the woman saw Samuel, she cried with a loud voice. . . ."

I lay for a moment listening. There were no noises now.

"And the king said unto her, What form is he of?
And she said, An old man cometh up; and he is covered
with a mantle. . . ."

A gorgeous bit of grue, I thought, and thoughtfully, I happened to look up. At the foot of my bed stood a grotesque, swollen figure.

"I rather hoped," it said, "that you wouldn't be asleep."

The voice was human enough, and after a moment of paralysis, the last of the Flowers took heart.

"I," said my visitor, "am Caspar Sarx. I regret that I was not downstairs to welcome you, for you, I believe, are Mr. Jonathan Flower."

He must have moved a little nearer the bed, for I saw him more clearly now—an immense man wrapped in a fantastic dressing robe, and on his head one of those Turkish smoking caps you find in Thackeray's drawings. A black mustache cut squarely across his face. Between his big white teeth, a long and lighted cigarette was clamped, the ash dropping from time to time on his clothing, the butt—when he removed it from his mouth—matted and wet. His voice was soporific, liquid, unguent.

"Observing a light in your room as I was passing by," said Dr. Sarx, "I ventured in to greet you."

(How do you pass by a room that is at the end of a corridor? And, don't Sarxes knock? But I had spoken nothing and continued to do so.)

"I hope," he went on, "that you will not find my children too demanding. *My* children?" (It was as if I had asked the question.) "Not mine precisely; rather the children of my poor dear niece. Nevertheless, mine in heart, mine in heart." His voice achieved the quintessence of saccharine. "How dear they are to me you will realize when I tell you that they have been here at Sexton's Prim for two years now. What with their mother, and their serving man, and those who meet my own small needs, and you"—he wet his lips—"we are quite a family." He actually executed what appeared to be a small caper.

"I'm looking forward to meeting them, sir. Tomorrow morning, I suppose?" I felt like an awful fool talking up to him from my bed like a patient to his doctor.

"Indeed, yes. Tomorrow morning it shall be. We breakfast about half-past eight—though I must confess that my own habits are not precisely regular, but in the Great Things one is not always one's own master, is one? No matter, no matter. You have been told our morning hours? Very well then. Good night. I hope you will be very happy here."

He faded backward into the darkness, and for all the light the door revealed as he opened and shut it in silence, he might have faded through the wall.

"I hope you will be very happy here"—his last words echoed in my ears. I wasn't sure.

I went to sleep at last with the small light burning.

Chapter

4

I awoke to bright sunlight and the smell of smoke. A small and bony boy in horn-rimmed glasses sat on the side of my bed, gently waving a catalpa bean. From its lighted end flowed a stream of acrid vapor.

"Awake thou that sleepest," said the little boy.

"And arise from the dead." The response, as I raised myself on both elbows, came from a little girl, standing by my open window. She was fatter than the boy but about the same height.

"It takes a great deal of purifying to wake him up," said she. "Perhaps he estivates like certain snails. And what about uncertain snails—when do they sleep? Excuse us. Good morning. He is Warburton. I am Lucy. You, we assume, are Mr. J. Flower."

"Most people call me Posy," I said. (In regular school relationships, a teacher should never allow the use of his first name. But this, I thought, was different.)

Lucy moved closer, her eyes appraising. "I like your pajamas," she told me.

"Could you possibly put that cigar out?" I asked her companion.

"Yes, do, Warburton. It stinks. Put it in the thing." Warburton left the room, but Lucy had another question.

"Are you a lickspittle?"

"I don't think so," I said. "Why should I be?"

"Munce says all male baby-sitters are lickspittles. They have to be, she says, or else they get the push. Have you ever gotten the push?"

"No—to tell you the truth, this is the first job like this I've had." I hastened to add some credentials. "I've been a camp counselor and a junior lifeguard, and I've fished the Orinoco —if that helps. I've been at school in Scotland, and I like to sail. I—"

Warburton, back in the room, interrupted. "Ask him how he is, Lucy."

His sister nodded. *"Ahvâl-e-sharif?"*

It was a common enough how-d'ye-do—if you happened to live in Asterabad. Luckily, I knew the conventional answer. *"Al-hamdo-lêllâh az eltefât-e-shomâ* (Praise be to God for your kindness)," I replied, "but I hope I'm not expected to improve your Persian." I had once spent two months in Isfahan, but that is scarcely long enough to learn Iranian.

For the first time, both of them appeared a mite impressed. And Lucy promptly returned to English.

"Come on down to breakfast, Posy. I think you should know that we are opposed to you, but we'll show you the ropes." She turned to her brother. "Let's go, Warburton. I'm dying to see what kind of clothes he wears."

I was relieved when they departed, leaving the choice to me.

What indeed *do* you wear on your first morning of "country house" employment? Most of my stuff was British (which is usually par for the sportswear course), but I didn't especially want to look like "Teddy Lester in the Fifth."

I compromised on a rather shaggy old school blazer, gray

22

flannels, and tennis shoes. But I needn't have worried, for at
the breakfast table Dr. Sarx was present, still in last night's
smoking cap and *jallabiyah*. A long cigarette depended from
his lips. With a suave and sweeping fork, he waved me good
morning.

"I believe you have met these two," he said. "Warburton
and Lucy Budding. Mrs. Budding is on the Prospect, readying
herself to sit."

I was growing a little used to the odd locutions of this family, but his last remark left me floundering.

"He means Munce is waiting for him to come and carve
her," Warburton explained. "They do it every morning."

Cereal appeared before me as a coffee-colored hand came
and went.

"This is Jamshid," said Dr. Sarx, "our managing director."
Jamshid was tall and slim, his face the color of dark cream, his
features aquiline and beautiful. On his head he wore a dark-
ish cap. The rest of him was elegantly covered in a long white
coat and the traditional Parsi *pyjamis*. He was definitely not
one of the assistants whom I had met the night before. Indeed, the night before, with its Grand Guignol accents,
seemed very far away. I was resolved to tell Dr. Sarx of my
shotgun welcome, but it seemed wiser to wait, at least until
the children were not with us.

"Have some egg," said Dr. Sarx. He took an enormous
mouthful himself, then, from some inner cavern, lanced two
rigid streams of smoke from his nostrils. "And coffee,
perhaps?" He cleared his throat and, using both hands, com-
bined a chunk of kidney and a long inhalation of tobacco.
Taking coffee to wash down the mixture, he polished his
mouth with a damask napkin. "Plans for the day, yes? They
are really yours to make. The children will show you about.
They are yours, I am sure, to command. Mrs. Budding will
want them—probably late in the afternoon. And of course, if

I am here, they come to me at six. Otherwise, I leave you to work out a schedule to suit yourselves." He swabbed his plate with a piece of sodden toast. And all the time he ate, the cigarette, now mostly ash, adhered to his lip—upper or lower as it suited his convenience. "You drive, of course?"

I explained that the cautious Commonwealth of Pennsylvania permitted me to drive—except between the hours of midnight and five in the morning. Dr. Sarx seemed interested in this form of license. "Ah yes, that will do nicely. Vickers—he met you at the plane last night—will show you which car to take, provided you need one. There is swimming right here in Gannet Bay, of course, and a boat or two." His fat white hand waved vaguely toward the south. "Warburton tells me you are an old sailor."

"Hardly that, Dr. Sarx, and of course I don't know your water at all."

"It's very safe," he assured me. "Very safe—inside the bars, that is. Though one thing I must warn you of. We have a fisherman down on the beach—a kind of long-term squatter. He has, I believe, some kind of hereditary right to the shack he keeps—and a right of way by one of our rougher trails. I do not trust the fellow, but he—er—came with the place. I have tried to dislodge him, but the inheritance laws of Massachusetts—especially when they deal with fishing—seem to be like those of the Medes and Persians."

I happened to look at Lucy. She was scowling darkly at her brother. Dr. Sarx appeared not to notice but sopped the remnant of his coffee. "One other thing," he said. "I had meant to ask you before: I suppose you have friends here and there on the Cape?" He seemed to wait for my answer with great eagerness.

This was grillwork, and I felt a little guilty, for one of my pleasures in accepting Dr. Sarx's employment was the fact that a very good friend of mine (female) had long been asking me to visit her family in West Orleans. West Orleans was probably a post office at most, I thought, but it couldn't be very far away.

"I do know some people whose mailing address is the same as yours, Dr. Sarx—West Orleans, I mean. There's a girl, you see"—at least I didn't say *this* girl—"there's a girl named Little—George Little, I think her father is—"

"Of course." He chomped thoughtfully on his last gobbet of kidney—like the late G. K. Chesterton munching a paradox. All in all, he didn't seem much pleased. "Of course. The Littles live off Windmill Way. *I* don't know them"—he managed to sound proud of it—"although, in a sense, they're neighbors. You've been over there, haven't you, Warburton?"

"Sure," said Warburton, "and I bet his girl's Chicken."

"Chicken?" asked Dr. Sarx.

Lucy giggled. "He doesn't mean she's scared. It's her name."

"Her nickname," I suggested. "After the chicken in the children's story, you know."

"Know what?" demanded Dr. Sarx.

"Why, Chicken Little!" Brother and sister came out with it in harmony, one voice a half tone higher than the other.

But further exegesis was cut off by an arrival. Here I ought really to pause and whet my pen. Through the French window she came, dressed in a clinging costume of dark blue. Her make-up, except for the red lips, was chalky white. She moved in a tinkle of golden ornaments and moved like music.

"Morning, Munce," said the children. (Or maybe it was Muntz—I never asked them to spell it.)

There were good mornings all around, and I was introduced to Mrs. Budding—"my niece Elizabeth"—and she smiled and was very gracious and told Warburton to wipe egg off his mouth.

"As I think I implied," intoned Dr. Sarx, "Elizabeth sits for me in the mornings. What a joy it is, my dear! And to what great objectives we have given ourselves!" He gleamed at her from behind his greasy napkin. "We have gotten well along with the *ilium sinister*—a fascinating locus but a most demanding one. And now, to work, to work."

The rest of us rose as the two departed. I had formed no clear impression of Mrs. Budding. With a less extreme make-up job, I told myself, she might come to life. I looked at each of the children in turn. Their faces were strangely sad.

"He paints?" I asked.

"No. Sculpts." Lucy was the spokesman. "Then, of course, he paints his sculptings. He carves, get it? That's why we call him Cutty—Cutty Sarx."

"When relations are unusually good," added Warburton, "we curry his favor by calling him 'uncle.' Munce, you see, is only a courtesy niece. None of us is of his blood."

Chapter

5

If the reader thinks that I have been touring him around a good bit, he may have some idea of what I went through that morning with the twins. They were neither rude nor proprietary. They simply were thorough, and our journey was conducted, if not with deference, at least with decency. Lucy continued to erupt with odd maturities: the child was obviously crammed with an enormous amount of irrelevant information. Warburton's knowledge proved equally exotic; his head, too, was planted with intellectual wild flowers of dubious bouquet.

By shortly after eleven, I had seen the duck pond and been shown the outside of the studio. The latter was a large one-story outbuilding, connected with the house by a considerable breezeway. The "Prospect" turned out to be an elevated ridge of close-cropped grass, but I saw no signs there of artist or model. At the opposite end of the house, a wing rose to windows above a barn-garage; I realized that one of the windows was mine. We walked around to the double doors that gave on the drive—there were three pairs of them, so that the whole front of the structure could be opened. I caught a glimpse of cars inside but nothing, happily, resembling a hearse. We did the downstairs of the house—living room, dining room, den, kitchen, and (from outside) the servants' rooms. One heavy oaken door at the rear of the house remained closed. It led, I was told, to the "lab."

"Lab for what?" I asked.

"It's where he invents things," Lucy volunteered. "It's his workshop, kind of—for secret things."

"In connection with the business," said Warburton.

"That reminds me," I ventured cagily. "I'm not sure that I understand what business your uncle's in." (Truth to tell, Charlie Vickers' explanation had left me unconvinced.)

The twins looked at each other and hesitated for a moment.

"He brings 'hours of tranquillity and days of comfort,' " said Lucy.

"She's quoting. She's quoting from the ads." Warburton was his sister's accuser.

"All right. So what if I am? I'll bet Posy's seen them plenty of times. Goodness knows, they're all over."

I had no recollection of the slogan, if such it was—but then maybe I read the wrong papers. Tranquillity suggested a pill.

"Is it a pill?" I asked.

"No," said Lucy. We were standing in the living room, and from the desk she handed me a small, discreet brochure. "DAYS OF TRANQUILLITY," it said, varying her quotation a little.

DAYS OF TRANQUILLITY

AND

YEARS OF COMFORT

LET SARX PLAN FOR YOU

AND FOR THOSE YOU LOVE

There followed the outline of an urn, delicate and double-eared. Underneath was the legend:

PEACE AT ANY PRICE

TAKES ON A NEW MEANING

I could no longer doubt my host's product, and there was a chilly note in his advertising that disturbed me. But I bluffed it out.

"Comfort stations?" I asked.

Lucy giggled. "Don't be silly," she said. (I was surprised that she knew the ancient term.)

"Rest homes?" It was a fine new guessing game.

"In a way." Obviously, I was getting warmer.

Warburton broke in. "Why don't you tell him? They're funeral parlors—Uncle Cutty's an undertaker. The biggest one going, I guess." The child looked at me doubtfully for approval. "He runs a chain," he added.

And I, be it confessed, experienced a spasm of relief. I hadn't been able to convince myself of the chauffeur's story; it had occurred to me persistently that he was covering something up. Now I was reassured. After all, I had nothing against undertakers. I remembered my father's saying that they were the most unselfish of public servants in their willingness to do a job most people would refuse. The obvious explanation of last night's adventure was corroborated and made sense. What more natural than for a gentleman of Dr. Sarx's profession to order up a sample casket now and then? And what more unobtrusive method of delivery than by night? His curious visit to my room I could put down to eccentricity. His manner, his costume, his menage—

No, it wouldn't quite work. The butterfly of suspicion was still alive in my stomach. It was illogical, I told myself—ridiculous!—but it still fluttered. Nobody had explained the gunshots. Nor do most people's chauffeurs arm young guests with .45's.

"He's *quite* famous." Warburton said it defensively.

"I'm sure he is." (I was thinking of those one hundred and sixty locations.) "And I suppose he's very busy."

"Yes," said Lucy, "but mostly with his carving really—sculpting, I mean."

"I'd like to see some of his work," I said.

Lucy pointed toward the door into the hall. "There's one," she said.

On the floor by the sill was a heavy stopper in the form of a cat, apparently worked in schist of the type they call hornblende. The sculpture was a dark green in color and pleasantly representational: if you knew a cat when you saw one, there was a cat. The left side of the creature was marked in black with what looked like a monogram.

I am a very poor bet when it comes to carving, but we have some odds and ends at home—picked up by my father here and there—and I seemed to remember just such a marking on a basalt statuette that came from the Nile Valley. I had knelt to examine Dr. Sarx's handiwork when a voice spoke almost in my ear. It wasn't the treble of the children but a deep and vibrant bass.

"The *tashrif* does not permit one to touch." Jamshid was standing tall at my side, having entered the room without a sound.

And since I hadn't been touching the schist—and couldn't have hurt it if I had—I said so. But here was a single-minded servant.

"Not permit to touch," he repeated.

We looked at each other for a moment, and I must confess that the man intrigued me. Those splendid eyes were honest if ever eyes were—nor was there anything of irritation in his reproof.

"I shan't," I said, "and thank you for the warning, Jamshid."

He bowed with a murmured *"Mota-shakker, âghâ,"* and I

30

had more than a notion where Lucy had picked up her Iranian.

"The chauffeur desires to see you, *âghâ*. At the window he is, there." Charlie Vickers was peering at me around a drapery.

"Want to go to the village?" he asked. "It's time for the mail."

"I'd like to," I told him, "but I've just lost the children. They were here a minute ago—"

"Gone down to the water. Payin' a visit to Snow, I betcha. Hee-hee. Good for them if Dr. Sarkuss don't catch 'em."

"Is Snow the fisherman?" I remembered Dr. Sarx's reference to a "squatter."

"Yup. Fine old fellow, too. Worth ten o' some people."

I didn't press him for an explanation. "You're sure they'll be all right?"

"Right? Right as rain. Go down to see the old man every day of their lives. Boss don't know of course. But he's an education all to himself, Mr. Snow is. And I tell you somethin', Mister Flower. When the kids are with him, or me, or Jamshid yonder, you don't have to worry." (I noticed with some curiosity that he had not mentioned their mother.) "Otherwise," he went on, "it's just as well to be on the lookout. I dunno, but there's some funny things goes on around here." He sighed, and I waited for a further revelation, but it was not forthcoming.

"Like rifle shots from the pine trees?" I prodded him.

"Hee-hee." He nodded. "Yup. Like that there and like some other things. Come on—let's get to the post office."

Try as I might, it seemed impossible to gain an explanation of the shooting. The armament on our side may have been innocent enough, but it was no blank that blew out our tire. For the time being, I abandoned my research.

Nothing much happened in the village. The business block

31

—if such it could be called—consisted of two garages and a general store. The post office window was suitably filled with post cards—surf, lobsters, and sea dogs, vying with beauty queens who looked less indigenous. A sign by a dirt road pointed to "Corporation Beach." In the sand that edged the pavement, white chips of oyster shell gleamed under the noonday sun.

Charlie picked up the mail. And, as I say, nothing much happened except for an odd conversation I had with one of the young men in overalls lounging in front of "Nickerson's Auto Clinic."

"You're the new feller over 't Sexton's Prim?"

I admitted it. Whereupon: "Sure must be fond of music," said he.

This was an approach I couldn't figure out. It's true that I am fond of music—at the time I was particularly sold on Peter, Paul, and Mary—but I failed to see how this addiction could be well known on the Cape.

Another question: "You're in the end room over the garage?"

"Yes," I said. "Why?"

"Well, that's where we strung all that wire—down the hall to the room. Dr. Sarx said you got some kind of fancy radio—said you'd fix it up." He chewed on a stalk of timothy. "Like to see it some time when you're done," he said.

Now I had brought no radio with me, nor had there been one in the room the night before. (I am, moreover, an extremely poor do-it-yourselfer). But on our return to Sexton's Prim, I found a neat little model beside my bed, plugged by the usual cord into a baseboard outlet. Only a careful search revealed the second, thinner wire, recently painted into the wall and disappearing in the corridor.

It was a bugging job all right. My father had described such installations all too often for me to mistake one. But for the life of me I couldn't see why anyone should want to listen in on *my* musings. Unless they expected me to have a good deal of company, they weren't likely to hear much besides a shoe-lace grunt or a midnight snore. Unless—I was sorely tempted: perhaps my hosts were starved for entertainment. If so, I could oblige. Assuming a slightly theatrical accent, I proceeded to soliloquize.

"Alas," I said—to nobody in particular—"alas, that I am brought to this!" Then, quickly, I turned into a gangster: "De rocks is hot," I said. "Karpus de Sharpus won't fence 'em. De fuzz is wise." I changed my voice again: "Greasy-puss is sendin' for a rod from Chi," I told my partner. "Love dat man," he replied. Then, in sugar-drop TV: "I shall read myself a story," I said.

I paused, as if looking for a book in my belongings. After a minute: "Once upon a time there were three bears. This"—I interrupted myself—"is a *good* story. Once upon a time there were three bears, and they lived in a house in the forest. There was Poppa Bear, and there was Momma Bear, and there was Little Bear."

I kept on for some time. Whoever was listening in could form his own opinion.

Chapter

6

But it was from this time forward that I felt uneasiness growing inside me. Granted, the curious method by which I'd been met had been partly explained. There remained, however, certain indefinables—words from Charlie, silences on the part of the children, and the personality, it had to be confessed, of Dr. Sarx himself. I felt as if the tangy coastal air were burdened by an onshore heaviness. Once, years before, I had known the same sensation when hurricane warnings went up.

What happened during the afternoon did nothing to settle my nervousness.

Four of us were playing tennis at Gannet Lodge, the Littles' summer place. The members of Chicken's household were our neighbors indeed by sea; but by land they were a lengthy roundabout of small roads distant. With Charlie's approval, I had left the children in Jamshid's keeping ("Maybe we go swimming, *âghâ!*") and helped myself to the Corvette. I found the lodge easily, its old gray shingles mounting to the tower of a disused windmill. To my surprise, the first person I encountered was Mrs. Budding, deep in porch-chair conversation with a man whom she introduced as Francis Torquil. Both of them were dressed for tennis (if you allow a man khaki shorts). Mrs. B. had on one of those white piqué things with a flaring skater's skirt; it became her quite as well as her morning *sari*.

After a moment or so, Chicken came out of the house with an armful of rackets and a handful of sandwiches.

"They're ham," she said. "Have one, Posy duck." I said thank you, no, I'd just had lunch, and how well you're looking. She was, too, her hair somewhat blonder than when I had seen her last (but of course that may have been the seashore air and sunshine) and her legs golden brown. Chicken may not be precisely a dish, but she constitutes a very sound *hors d'oeuvre*. Besides, she has always been good with a racket.

I've never been overly fond of mixed doubles, but if a girl has a strong serve and useful ground strokes, you can forgive a lot in the way of volleying. Mrs. Budding, who—thank the Lord!—did not insist that I call her by her first name (of all perverted adult fancies!), turned out to be a steady player, a bit patty-cake but with a good sense of direction. Her partner —at least in the warm-up—looked very good indeed, a real stylist with the follow-through that my father always attributes to George Agutter, his old-time pro at Forest Hills.

Just as we were ready to start, there came an interruption in the form of Chicken's grandmother. Of this lady I shall have considerably more to write, but she demands an introduction. Gray wispy hair fluttered above a pink face in which the eyes and—I regret to say—the nostrils were always faintly wet. Mrs. Little looked as if she had just been crying or else was just about to begin. And when you add to these features a vague weaving of the hands and a *most* uncorseted garment of lavender chiffon—folds upon folds—you have the picture.

Or almost all of it. As she came toward us from the house, she seemed at first to be garlanded with flowers, but a nearer glance revealed that her decorations were—tomatoes! Small tomatoes in a coronet around her head—one or two drooping to her shoulders—and a veritable plastron of tomatoes sweeping across her front like a bloody Sam Browne belt from neck to waist. In the good Cape breeze, her garments fluttered like her hands.

Chicken introduced me, and her grandmother looked me over with a radiant smile. Her wet eyes glistened, and she seemed delighted to encounter Youth in Action.

"Lovely," she said. "Lovely for you to be here. Now is the day of youth's delight." Her voice was thin and high with the clear enunciation of stage training. Aimlessly, she plucked at the nearest tomato in her corsage.

    " 'Flung roses, roses riotously with the throng.' "

She quoted *con amore*. *"You* know," she said—" 'The viol, the violet, and the vine.' Curious how he liked v's, wasn't it? You know Dowson, of course?"

I half expected her to produce him, viol and all, but I merely established the fact that I had read the works of Cynara's admirer.

"Here," she said. "Here—for a garland." And removing the chaplet of vegetables from her head, she proceeded to advance on me, holding the tomatoes before her in the form of a noose.

Chicken came to the rescue. "Not now, Goosie, not when we're just going to play. Save it for him—there's a good girl. To the victor belong the spoils. And he isn't the victor yet."

It's queer the way you remember some games as if you'd just played them. In my mind's eye, I can see each point of that day's tourney blow by blow. Chicken won her serve. Mrs. Budding won hers—thanks to Mr. Torquil's value at the net. I made Chicken take what they used to call the Australian position—playing net on my side of the court—and we were well into a pleasant fracas when the second interruption came.

This time, it was serious. Out of the corner of my eye, I had seen a maid in conference with Mrs. Little. That good lady, just as our game ended, fluttered across the court and began talking to Mrs. Budding. I stepped over the net, and Chicken came hurrying around the winding post.

There had been an accident at Sexton's Prim. Lucy was hurt. Her mother and I were wanted immediately.

Back at Dr. Sarx's house, nobody seemed to know quite how it had happened. Jamshid and Warburton had been following Lucy up from the shore—a distance not much more than a quarter of a mile—when they flushed a couple of bobwhites and started off in rather fatuous pursuit. The next thing they knew was that somewhere ahead of them Lucy was screaming.

She had reached the front of the garage apparently (where a board incline led from the building to the drive) and was facing back in the direction from which she had come when the brakes on the pick-up truck somehow slipped and the heavy vehicle came rolling out on top of her. The off fender caught her in the leg, she was tossed to one side, and the truck came to a stop against some rocks a few yards farther on. What might have happened if she had been standing in the center of its path, we didn't like to think about.

Of course, by the time we got there, the victim was tucked in bed and the doctor had spoken his word of reassurance. Nothing was broken, it seemed, and besides some scrapes and bruises, Lucy's chief symptoms consisted of bewilderment. By the time the doctor left, denying any need for X-ray, everybody was much relieved.

And curiously uninterested, I thought—especially in what seemed to me the principal mystery: granted faulty or forgotten brakes, how did the truck get started moving?

Torquil had driven Mrs. Budding home, and she was busy with her daughter when I carefully backed the Corvette I had been driving into the garage. There was ample room to set the whole length of the car well within bounds, and the same thing, I was certain, would have been true of the truck, now undergoing a close inspection by Charlie Vickers. One of the dark assistants stood by, watching him.

Undoubtedly, the big old building had once been a barn. Up a side wall, rungs led to an obvious hayloft, and a rope still hung from its block, ready for future bales. What drew me most was the collection of odd objects hung against the back or propped on firebreaks in mad confusion. High up, a moose's head—demoted, no doubt, from the house—sneered down at children's sleds, bright painted buoys, stuffed ducks, odd oars, a rudder, and a stringless ukelele. Sweeps for a one-man shell stood in the corner partly veiled by yards of weathered net. Over my head as I looked up, suspended from the rooftree hung—of all things!—a schoolroom swivel chair (of first-grade size, I thought), complete with iron foot and base. This item of décor was flanked by a pair of acetylene headlights from some ancient car, their brass now black and green with salty weather.

The collection deserved another and more thorough going over. But for the present, I was chiefly interested in the lower portions of the barn—and particularly the floor of the middle stall where the truck had stood.

There were footprints aplenty, but the weathered wood took impressions less immediate than one is apt to find on either asphalt or concrete. Toward the back of the parking space, high heels had wandered; farther forward, some sort of rubber-studded walking boot had left its pug marks in the greasy dust. The rippled pad of tennis shoes was everywhere about. Over the sill and down the short ramp, truck treads had written a repeated pattern. It was possible only to assume that the latest tire tracks were on top.

I didn't know what I was looking for, anyway.

"Charlie," I called, "was it the brakes?" During my search the assistant had taken himself off.

"Can't find a thing," said Charlie, his voice coming from the underbody. The truck was a Russian import—rather a rare bird, I thought—a Moskvitch 430 with a stick shift. "Get in there," Charlie told me, "and pull that handle." So for another half an hour, I pumped the brake for him while he checked drums and bands and rods.

"Absolutely all right," he announced at last, wiping the sweat from his brow. "Foot brake's O.K., too—not that that would have made any difference. One thing though"—he ran his hand through a drooping forelock and looked at me with Will Rogers' wryness—"I don't leave no cars in neutral, nor trucks neither. This here's got four speeds forward, and I been lockin' European shifts for years."

I let that one go, though it occurred to me that in these days of automatic transmission, stick shift, floor shift, and all the variations, even the most experienced driver could get mixed up between cars.

"Don't explain nothin', anyway." Charlie's face was almost bitter, and the giggle had quite gone from him. "When I put a car away, I put it away—brake on, wheels locked, *in* gear, and keys *out*. Look." He showed me the full ring drawn from his pocket. "I swear I plain can't understand it."

"Well," I said. "I'm certain nobody's blaming you, Charlie." But he shook his head forbiddingly.

"Wait till *he* comes home." He jerked his thumb toward the house. "Never can tell what *he'll* think."

"Doesn't he know yet?"

"Been away ever since lunch. Took the Cadillac and drove himself."

A new thought had come to me. "Has anybody asked where everybody was when the thing happened?"

"No. Don't believe so. I was in the kitchen talking to Mrs. Simpson."

Mrs. Simpson was the cook. "That lets two of you out," I said.

He looked at me sharply. "You think somebody—was involved in this here?"

39

"I don't think even Russian cars start themselves. Somebody must have been monkeying around. Fooling, I suppose —but fooling with that gear shift. If Warburton hadn't been chasing quail—"

"Warburton wouldn't touch no car. I got him trained on that. He's a monkey, like all of 'em his age, but he wouldn't fool with no levers. Still, guess you're right about its bein' somebody. Truck was in neutral when it hit these rocks."

"It was? You're certain?"

He scratched his head. "No, I ain't certain 'cause I don't know who was at the truck first. I heard Lucy screamin' and beat it round the garage. I saw where the truck had landed but went straight to Lucy. Seems like everybody was around right away."

Mrs. Simpson, it appeared, had followed him directly from the kitchen. The assistants had arrived, as he remembered, from the direction of the south woods. But Charlie didn't really know the order of their arrival. He had been too much concerned about the little girl to pay much attention.

I totted the roll call over on my fingers. "I don't suppose the fisherman—what's his name? Snow?—was in sight?"

"Funny you should ask that. He never comes up to the house—not since him and Dr. Sarkuss had words. But he was here this afternoon. Hee-hee." (Charlie was getting back to normal.) "Came up through the woods. Must have followed Jamshid and Warburton."

"What did he do? Did he say anything—anything unusual? Did he have any theories about how it happened—anything like that?"

Charlie thought for a minute, then climbed into the cab of the Moskvitch. "Nope," he said, "he didn't say a word. Just waited till we seen Lucy wasn't hurt real bad. Didn't say a word."

He slammed the truck door shut and started the engine. The sound of it was unimpaired.

"He didn't say nothing," Charlie repeated, leaning from the window and speaking with intensity. "He just stood. And just before he went back in the woods, he turned clean round and shook his fist at the house."

Chapter

7

I decided that Mr. Snow would be worth a visit, but remembering my nanny-like duties, I went to look for Warburton. That young man was sitting at the foot of the stairs, dismally trying to splice a broken shoelace. Between us we managed to knot it, and he agreed that a trip to the beach would be acceptable.

"She's really all right, isn't she?" He jerked his thumb in the direction of his sister's room upstairs.

"I'm sure she is," I told him. "Do you think we ought to call on her?"

"Oh, I've been. She talked and everything. You know how she talks." I did. "Anyway, she's asleep now. Mrs. Simpson's sitting with her."

Vague as I was about the duties of my post, I hardly thought that part of the job was to sit by at naptime. "You'll have to show me the way, then. Do we take trunks?"

"Got mine on," said Warburton, indicating his faded khaki shorts. "I just go in in these. It won't be awfully good tide, though."

He was right. It wasn't awfully good tide, but the afternoon sun shone brightly on a vast crescent of beach, and the wavelets of the bay twinkled like brilliants on a blue-green dress. Near us was a silver shack.

I can't describe it any other way, for the vertical planking of which it was built had weathered so many winds that its sides had a soft, metallic sheen. Near the groundline of the walls, broad swathes of sun-dyed color blended with the gray —test splashes of boat paint, doubtless, brightly borne on many a hull but here subdued like the tints inside a pearl.

An antiquated pair of railway tracks, half buried in the sand, led down from the shack into the water. On the landward side, a door stood open, silver like the rest, and over it a whale-shaped sign, the letters barely visible:

FREDk SNOW
LOBSTERS

To bear out this boast, a number of dried-out pots were piled beside the shack and draped with nets. Two boats, an inboard dinghy and an old-time cat—both stripped of gear—rested on weary-looking horses. A square-end pram was beached at the water's edge.

With his back to the bay, Warburton pointed to a bluff above the sandy trail that we had followed.

"See the battery?" he said.

I followed his pointing finger and made out first one, then two, brass cannon, almost hidden by masses of beach plum and blueberry. The pieces were six-pounders by the look of them.

"What on earth are *they* for?" I asked.

"Put there long ago," said Warburton. "Lucy and me— Lucy and I—keep 'em shiny." And sure enough, the sun glinted where the brasswork was not overgrown. "We shoot 'em at buoys and things—Fourth of July and like that. Round stones work fine." He recited:

> " '*O well for the fisherman's boy*
> *That he shouts with his sister at play!'*

"—Tennyson, you know." He indicated a break in the sweeping shoreline, some hundreds of yards to the north. "Up there is Littles' Cove. That's where their brook comes down into the bay. It's a wonderful place for mummies. We seine for 'em. Have you ever seined for bait?"

I didn't answer because we were about to have company. From the shoreside door of the silver shack emerged a figure almost as silvery. Only the deep mahogany of hands and face —and, as he drew nearer, the piercing blue of wise old eyes— relieved the drabness of his clothing. The crushed-down canvas hat and shooting shirt had paled from khaki to off-white; the denim trousers were a sandy gray; even the sea boots were so salt-encrusted as to have no color.

"Hi there, Warburton!" (He pronounced it "Wabbit'n.") "Who's your friend?" asked Mr. Snow.

One hears a good deal about the dour New Englander. Grant Wood's Gothic faces really belong—in many people's thinking—to the coasts and hinterlands of Maine and Massachusetts. And at very first glance, one might have taken for severity in Mr. Snow what was actually strength, and for aridity what was dry humor. He was long, somehow, without being tall and lean without being cadaverous. When he spoke, it was the lobsterman's idiom, but the whole town of Orleans knew that he could talk like a professor from Harvard College if he chose to.

Warburton proceeded to introduce me: "This is—er—Posy Flower—*Mr.* Posy Flower. He's here to keep an eye on us— Lucy and me. Lucy got run over, did you know?" (It was scarcely a recommendation.)

"I heard somethin'," said Mr. Snow.

Warburton was gazing seaward, searching, I thought, the long low island that lay half a mile offshore. But—

"Where's *Bluejacket*?" he asked.

"I brought her in, son. Want to check the transom. Looks like somebody's been foolin' with her. *Bluejacket,*" he explained to me, "is the dory these two youngsters use a-fishin'."

"I didn't know there was anything wrong with the transom." Warburton was still looking seaward. "Oh! Whose is that? She's new!"

A tall sloop was standing in to the bay. Without waiting for an answer, Warburton ran down the beach and entered the shallow water, almost as if he were trying to reach the distant craft. I followed him as far as the first clear curling flounces of incoming tide. In the shallows, fiddler crabs were on parade, their bow-arms raised and waving. A submarine symphony, I thought.

"Sarx keeps a cruiser over t' the Harbor," said Mr. Snow. "Calls her the *Queen of Sheba!* Too much power to my thinkin', but that's the way they likes 'em nowadays. . . . Come here, Wabbit'n. Something here I want to show you." And of the sloop—"She'll make t'other side th' island."

(I realize that I'm laying on the dialect a bit thick, but the voices of these people come back to me the way they sounded, and to put them into perfectly straight English seems a kind of disloyalty.)

"Take a look at that clamp, Wabbit'n. What've I told you about clamps?" Mr. Snow had led us around to the far side of the shack, where a clinker-built dory lay snug against the building. A seven-and-a-half horse outboard was mounted on the stern, where letters (in appropriate color) spelled out *Bluejacket.*

"Take a look at that clamp."

Warburton grasped one of two handles protruding inboard from the transom. The metal collar-plate rattled against wood, and the screw of the clamp turned easily.

The boy looked up, and if I'd known him well enough to judge, I'd have said there was a shadow of fear in his eyes. At any rate, he was puzzled.

"*I* didn't leave it that way." He tried the other handle with similar results. "You must've loosened it, Mr. Snow."

"No, sir. Found it like that at the mooring. Dang motor near fell off when I towed her in. Somebody was mighty careless—or else he didn't want you fishin', Wabbit'n. Any idea who don't want you fishin'?"

This time there was a definite tremor in the boy's voice. "No, Mr. Snow. Course not. But it would have been a nuisance—the motor coming off, I mean."

"Surely would." Mr. Snow indicated a white buoy riding at considerable distance from the shore. "Twelve foot of water there at low tide. I believe you, Wabbit'n. You know too much to leave a motor loose like that." His tone changed to one of brisk authority. "You run down to the cove now and see if there's any bait fish. Tide's makin'."

Warburton scampered off, glad apparently to quit the neighborhood of the molested *Bluejacket*. Mr. Snow watched him for a distance, then said to me, "I didn't show him the chain."

Fastened at one end to a ring bolt in the decking, and at the other to the motor, was a rubber-covered safety chain.

"Look-a-here," said Mr. Snow, fingering a length of it. One link was almost parted, the rubber eaten to the metal and the metal itself cut nearly through.

Ideas began to form. "You mean that somebody's done this deliberately—that somebody's out to spoil the kids' fun?"

"That's one way of puttin' it." He paused. "Tell you what, young man. I've got to speak my mind and—considerin' the way things are with me up at the house—I might as well speak it to you. I think this here sabotage is some crazy landsman's idea not just of spoiling the kids' fun but of harmin' the kids."

"But how?" I protested. "The way this is rigged, all you'd have to do is give the lanyard a couple of yanks—and the whole motor'd fall off."

"Surely it would. Surely it would. But suppose some feller don't know much about boats and clamps and lanyards. Suppose he thinks because he's only cut the chain part way that nothin'll happen till they've got themselves well out. And supposin' he's heard tales o' tide and rips and that kind o' business—"

"But they could always row," I suggested.

"Sure-ly. And there's always oars in the dory—'cept when I brought her in this afternoon."

Chapter

8

Mrs. Budding, I thought that evening at dinner, took a curiously passive interest in her children. (Having lost my own mother when I was a baby, I am always especially interested in female parents.) I admired her pleasant way with Lucy—of whose misfortune she made neither too much nor too little—and I sensed that both children respected her judgment, not sentimentally but rather as if they had thought the matter over, weighed her, as it were, in an objective balance, and found her generally satisfactory.

Certainly, she made a most attractive hostess as she sat in the doctor's usual place at the head of the table. For the evening she wore a summery frock of yellow gauzy stuff.

It was a late meal: we had awaited word from Dr. Sarx, and he finally phoned—apparently from Boston—to say that he would not be back until the next morning. Accordingly, the four of us were waited on in rather lonely dignity by Jamshid, who brought to us in turn a chilled white consommé, lobster knuckles on rice, a good mixed salad, and minted orange.

Mrs. B., as I say, was a gracious if somewhat unexciting hostess. It was a pleasure, however, simply to look at her; and Lucy, though a mite subdued, rivaled her brother with conversational gambits.

"Posy," she asked, "what do you know about helium deposits in the United States? I've been reading about them for the past two hours, and I've decided to build a dirigible. I'll blow up one of those cigar balloons of Warburton's and use it as a template—cover it with papier-mâché, you know, and then when it bursts, I'll have my shape—the bag, that is—all safe and sound. An adequate supply of helium is my chief problem."

"I think," said Mrs. Budding, "that one of your chief problems is your French. Can we start working on that tomorrow morning, Posy? With both of them, I mean."

"We shan't speak a word of anything else from after breakfast on," I said.

"Till when?" Warburton wanted to know.

"Till I run out of conversation." I was thinking of my French vocabulary—a far from inexhaustible asset—but Lucy drew a broader inference.

"I don't think you'd ever run out, Posy—at least not in *ordinary* languages. Never mind, *dar chand mâh digar khob amukhté bâshid.*" Behind me Jamshid snorted briefly; I hadn't thought him capable of laughter. Mrs. Budding looked annoyed. I recognized that Lucy's Iranian had something to do with learning "in a few months."

We heard the phone ring in the hall. Jamshid was back in a minute with word that the call was for me. Should he take the message? I hesitated—it might be Chicken, of course—but on a hunch I said no. If Mrs. Budding would excuse me, I would take the message myself. It turned out to be one of J. Flower's wiser decisions.

"A telegram for Mr. Jonathan Flower, Sexton's Prim, West Orleans, Mass.," said the operator's flat, incurious voice. "Sir, there are a couple of words here that I don't understand. Shall I spell them?"

"Yes," I said, a pleasant suspicion rising inside me. "Spell them when you come to them."

49

"I will spell them, sir. The message follows: 'Australia postponed joining you special delivery hush.' Then come these words, sir: 'H-A-S-T-A'—and then 'L-U-E-G-O.' Do you understand, sir? There is no signature, but the telegram was handed in at New York, New York."

Jamshid was somewhere in the hall, and I didn't repeat the message. Did I understand? "Thank you very much," I said. "No, you needn't mail a copy. It's quite clear. Thank you."

I had as long a time as it took to regain the dining room in which to devise a report on my call.

"Wire from a friend of mine," I said quite truthfully. "He's planning to be down on the Cape in a day or two."

"Oh, how nice," said Mrs. Budding, vaguely hospitable. "I hope he'll come and see us. Where is he staying?"

Again I was the soul of honesty: "I'm not sure," I said, "and I don't believe he's quite sure either. But he'll probably look us up."

I was particularly certain because I knew that the telegram came from my father. The Spanish sign-off was a code that he used—only with me. Once upon a time it had been cracked—appropriated, as it were—by an Amalekite. But that was once upon a time. For the present, I had no doubt of its validity. Why the Australian junket had been canceled only goodness (and the State Department) knew. What "special delivery" meant I had no idea. "Hush" was obvious.

Knowing him as I did, one other fact was obvious, too: someone or something in the neighborhood of Sexton's Prim had aroused his professional attention. Summer resorts were not his dish, and he had seen me lately for a longer time than was usual. So far as I knew, he had no acquaintance in my Cape Cod ménage; but I remembered one thing he had said: "That chap Sarx sounds very interesting."

The children had gone to play chess, and Mrs. B. and I were lingering over our coffee when the next major act of that extraordinary night's performance split the air.

It was a scream, a long, wailing scream from somewhere just outside the dining room. Silence followed for a moment; then we distinctly heard the patter of running feet, a soft sound on the flagstones of the terrace.

Rash intrusion is a habit that I generally avoid, but in this case there wasn't much choice. The French windows were standing open to the night's warm air. Without a word I darted through the nearest of them. The screen banged behind me as I peered first to my left (where I thought the cry had come from), then to the right. For a moment my eyes, unused to the darkness, saw nothing. Then beside the terrace, I made out a blotch of shadow, which was no mere incidental landscaping. In the edge of the light thrown from the house, a man lay still and silent on the grass.

The thought occurred to me that the marauder—after the fashion of his kind—might yet be lurking in the bushes. Or, indeed, that the apparent victim might be nothing of the sort. It was with wary glances, therefore, fore and aft—and with that "pricking of my thumbs" of which Mr. Shakespeare writes so eloquently—that I crept nearer the fallen one.

It was one of the assistants, and he lay face down, an arm thrown out as if in belated defiance. The white shirt *cum* blue apron uniform comprised what I had seen him wear the night before.

Gingerly, I put my hand on his back, a little below the left shoulder blade. There was a noticeable pulse, and as someone from indoors turned on a floodlight, I saw with relief that he bore no obvious wound. Behind me, I heard footsteps.

It was Jamshid with an electric flash, hardly necessary now. The blade of the beam caught the ground beside the victim and revealed a red fez, tumbled from his head apparently in the attack.

"Coshed," I said. "Coshed right here," and I guided the beam of Jamshid's flashlight to the back of the man's head. The skin was not broken, but touching him as lightly as I could, I felt a lump beginning to assert itself behind his ear.

For the second time in five minutes, the silence of the night was shattered.

"Ali! Ah-li!" Jamshid's voice was a rich baritone, waking the echoes with its resonance. "Ali!"

There followed some shouted Arabic that was too fast for me. A crackling in the underbrush, and the other assistant emerged into our path of light, his face a mask of fear. Jabbering, he knelt beside his colleague. And as I stood behind him, an unidentifiable impression struck my mind. It was one of those experiences you know have taken place: by the time you sense them, they are already lost. So mine was gone in an instant. I didn't know what I had seen; only knew that I *had* seen something.

Ali looked up with great uncertainty at me. I hoped that Jamshid was reassuring him—and making it perfectly clear that it was not I who had bashed his buddy. Whatever it was they said to each other, it seemed to quiet Ali down; between them the two picked up their fallen comrade and carried him into the house. I followed with the flashlight, thinking that in a way this was a repetition of the night before.

"They've taken him to his room," Mrs. Budding said. She was standing, movie-fashion, with her back to the far wall of the living room, a twin at either hand. "Was it—was it a burglar, do you think?"

I could think of a good many answers to that one, but I forbore.

"Perhaps I'd better phone the doctor," I suggested, "and then the police?"

She nodded in an absent sort of way, and I wondered whether she was in partial shock. The children had not spoken but watched with wise wide eyes.

I tried the doctor's number, but the line was busy. Reporting this failure to the living room, I encountered silence.

Finally, Warburton remarked—apparently of the assistants—"They never say very much."

I started back to the hall when Jamshid, the imperturbable, regained our side.

"I am happy to say, *khanoûm*, that Butrus is regaining consciousness. It is unfortunate but true that he has an antagonism—I speak not precisely—he has one who dislikes him in the village, one who has made threats to effect a fighting—"

It was remarkable how closely Mrs. Budding followed the butler's words. I was certain at once that there was some special link between these two—not the snake-and-rabbit business, nor anything disreputable—but a confidential relationship far beyond that of mistress and servant.

"The miscreant has come," Jamshid went on. "He has come, and without doubt, he has gone. And Butrus is beaten. Yet for the sake of his face—of his honor, it appears—this Butrus desires no doctor, lest the sad news of his downfall become common talk and his enemy thus triumph twice. Of this incident he wishes—how shall we say?—that not manybody know. As for the police, *khanoûm*—you were thinking of the police?" He included me in his glance.

"You will remember perhaps, *khanoûm*, that there was—as Dr. Sarx, the *tashrif* himself, has told us—some small trouble when Butrus and Ali entered the country—a detail, I believe, as to the rules of immigration. The poor Butrus! He and his brother are most anxious to avoid a confronting of the officials —if the *khanoûm* would be so considerate—"

He was an able pleader, and for all I knew, his story might be straight as a string. It was certainly possible that the two assistants had wet-backed their way into the country. It was not unlikely that one of them should be at feud with a village swain. In any event, Jamshid had made his impression on Mrs. Budding, and she offered but a token of resistance.

"But, Jamshid, if what you say is true—that is, I mean if

Butrus's story is true—about the man in the village, why, he will keep coming, won't he? We don't want a running battle here at Sexton's Prim. You know how Dr. Sarx feels about publicity—"

"Exactly, *khanoûm*. It is for the *tashrif's* feelings that I am especially concerned. As for this village fellow, I swear, *khanoûm*, that if you will leave the matter to me, you shall be no more troubled. I myself shall keep guard—"

"Very well." Her tone held relief as well as dismissal. "I think I'll put the children to bed," she said.

The crunch of tires sounded on the drive. With a quick look out the front window, Mrs. B. whisked her charges off, and I heard their several footsteps receding up the stairs.

I wondered whether we were receiving guests or whether— the thought crossed my mind—Mrs. Simpson had taken matters into her own hands while we were talking and made a back-stairs phone call for the cops.

Both guesses were wrong. Out in the driveway stood the very vehicle that had brought me to Sexton's Prim, and as I watched, Charlie Vickers climbed from the driver's compartment, slammed the hearse door, and started up the front steps. I met him on the porch.

"So it's a nightly delivery," I said. "How nice! Just like the morning milk."

"Hee-hee. Just about that. And it's a fancy one tonight. Those bronze jobs comes heavy. Where's the two lads?"

I told him about our visitation and, between clucks and simpers, he expressed what seemed to me to be a very mild concern. Jamshid's tale of Butrus's village foe left him especially unmoved.

"Maybe so," he said. "Maybe so. I never heard of no such feller, but it could be." He looked back at the hearse. "Reckon we'll have to rassle the thing ourselves—us and Alley-oop. Needs more'n two—even without a passenger—

54

and this baby feels almost like it had one. Hee-hee. They was cussin' at it plenty down to station."

It was not the fear of physical exertion that made me hesitate. To be perfectly frank, I had never touched a casket in my life, and empty though I knew it to be, I was reluctant to start with this one.

"Jamshid'll help," I suggested. But Charlie shook his head.

"Wouldn't touch it with a ten-foot pole," he told me. " 'Gainst his religion or somethin'. Why, he won't even go into the lab. I'll fetch Alley-oop."

He strode past me into the hall, and at that instant a fearful caterwauling burst from the back parts of the house. It was Ali in the solo bit with contrapuntal offerings from Jamshid. The two of them came through a door from the kitchen quarters, Ali wringing his hands in patent distress, Jamshid spouting Arabic at more than ordinary speed.

"This creature of the Nile has lost the key to the laboratory," Jamshid said. (He pronounced the final word in British fashion.) "He says that Butrus had it, but Butrus, whom we have now undressed, has it not at all."

"The key? Why do we need a key to the lab?" I asked.

"The—er—receptacle, the case which has been delivered" —Jamshid steered around the word—"it must be placed in the working room, where the others are kept. This is the *tashrif's* order; and it is only the two—Ali and Butrus—who possess entrée. I myself," he added hurriedly, "am forbidden."

"You're forbidden to enter the laboratory?" I had thought of Jamshid as a major-domo without limits.

"I am forbidden—here." He touched his breast. "I have no part with the things of death." (As for this last bit, I was with him all the way. I had no part with them either—at least I hoped so.)

But Charlie was of a different mind. "Come on, Posy," he

said. "You'n' me and Alley-oop'll get the thing. We can't let it sit out there all night. Bad for the eppydermis. Hee-hee. 'Sides, I have to get the wagon back—all the way to Hyannis. C'mon."

"There is no entrance, I insist." Jamshid was unalterably negative.

"Then we'll leave her in the back hall." Charlie turned and made for the back hall. I was obviously in for a spot of pall-bearing whether I liked it or not.

And as Charlie had said, the casket was amazingly heavy. With Ali straining at the forward end, the chauffeur and I each took (or should I say *under*took?) a corner of the rear. Among the three of us, we barely managed the steps and, as Jamshid politely held doors for us, staggered along the hall to the back of the house. Outside the laboratory door, we set our burden down. I had been very little in this portion of the house, and I noticed for the first time that the doctor's private workroom was protected by a large and elaborate lock. Like all such barriers to access, it had a fascination for me, and I wondered how long it would take my father to cope with it.

Charlie was mopping his brow.

"Sure you ain't got the key?" He glared at Ali. "Nor your buddy neither?"

Ali shook his head, eyes wide with fright and misery.

"Then we'll have to leave her right here." Charlie indicated an eight-foot space across a doorway to the rear. "His Nibs'll be back in the morning. *He*'ll have a key all right, but he's going to be mad about this goings-on."

We three willing workers proceeded to stow the casket neatly on the floor against the wainscoting. It looked for all the world like a metal settee.

"Perhaps," came Jamshid's Oriental unction, "it might be overlaid."

Under his arm he held an Eastern rug—from its lack of pile I took it to be a *kilim*. Charlie spread it over the casket, first with a careless flip, then with tidy tugs and straightenings. He made an odd sort of lady decorator.

"How's that look?" he asked. "Granny's trunk and a Turkish drugget. Who would know that here lies—"

"It is better," said Jamshid, "that the thing be covered. It is better *here*"—and again he touched his breast with a gesture almost ceremonial. "If there is anything I can do for you, *âghâ*—?"

"No," I told him. "I'm for bed."

"And I," said Charlie, "must take the wagon back." He pulled a watch from the pocket of his trousers. "Five to eleven. Hope I don't wake you coming home."

"You will not wake me," promised Jamshid. "I shall be on watch."

This assurance seemed to call for no comment, and I decided that before I went to bed, I would call up Chicken. There had been some talk of my popping over to the Littles' in the course of the evening. Perhaps it was not strictly truthful when I told her that the duties of my job had proved too strenuous. Unappreciatively, she said, "I'll bet you're holding hands with Madame Budding." Then she hung up.

Chapter

9

Once again, I couldn't sleep. I tried First Samuel, but the Amalekites spoiled Ziklag and David smote them so hard that I felt wider awake than ever. The night was quiet except for a soft wind in the stirring poplars. At a quarter to one, I heard the truck come in (I was almost exactly above the garage), and sundry noises told of Charlie Vickers making for bed in the servants' wing.

It occurs to me that I have not described the layout of the house except to say that it was rambling. It was all of that, for the downstairs of what must have been the original dwelling was connected to the garage structure by a one-story sequence of side-by-side bedrooms. These were the quarters occupied by Charlie, Jamshid, and the two assistants. (Mrs. Simpson, it seemed, came and went by the day.) From the servants' hall, the stair led up to my corridor, and out of this the children's rooms opened across from each other. An odd arrangement, so I thought—and later learned that till my coming Mrs. Budding had slept where I did now.

Or rather, where I didn't, for although I resolutely turned off the light and played the back nine at Oakmont hole by hole—which is my method of counting sheep—sleep would not come.

Now and then I thought I heard a footstep in the house but put it down to ancient timbers or the children stirring in their rooms. The wind had freshened, and a slow, reiterated whisper spoke of rising tide along the beaches of the bay.

I had just about decided to give the Amalekites one more fling when the total darkness of the room was broken. There had been no sound of switch or footfall, but sitting up in bed, I saw a streak of light, faint but definite, along the crack under my door.

I slipped out of bed and managed a silent passage across the room. The keyhole was large and unobstructed as I applied my eye. Standing not six feet from me, silhouetted in the glow of his own flashlight, was the tall, unmistakable figure of Jamshid.

As I watched, he moved away, then stopped again. His long white coat showed light against the darkness, and he seemed to be listening at Warburton's door. Across the hall he stopped again, as if expecting sound effects from Lucy's room.

A peculiar kind of patrol, I told myself—scarcely the faithful *khidmutgar* on guard, nor yet the hound across the door. He had spoken of "keeping watch" but had surely been referring to a watch against invaders from without. I wondered whether there were time clocks in the house.

His light began to flicker toward the stair. Consumed with curiosity, I opened my door a crack, slipped through, and proceeded to follow the Parsi butler on his strange patrol.

I understand that when you are older, you are less apt to embark on such capers. Or that, at any rate, you take thought for the morrow and that sort of thing. But as I padded after Jamshid through the dark of Sexton's Prim, the morrow didn't mean a thing; nor did it even enter my head—I'm ashamed to say—that I was leaving my charges, Warburton and Lucy, to their own innocent devices. For me, it was simply a case of "follow the gleam."

I stayed well behind till Jamshid's light began to disappear downward. Then I quickened my pace and reached the head of the stairs just in time to see it moving through the dog run past the servants' bedrooms. Perhaps the poor man, having reached the completion of his rounds, was about to retire.

But no. The flashlight cast its eerie circle well ahead of him into the main part of the house. And he was moving with a purpose: there was no stopping now to look or listen. Jamshid knew exactly where he was going.

To the left, into the principal hallway; on, in swift reconnoiter, past the den to the dining room; back again, almost catching me, to where we had carried the casket earlier in the evening; back, till the circle of light grew small and clear—on the lock of the laboratory door.

For a second or two, he stood stock still; then he turned quickly, and I sheltered myself beside a bookcase just as his flashlight swept the dog run. A single arc in that direction seemed to satisfy him, but I noticed that he fixed the casket briefly with his beam. Somehow or other, the Oriental rug had slipped from its moorings, and one end of the metal case was uncovered. At the time I gave the matter no thought, for I was fascinated by Jamshid's next move. From the pocket of his coat, he took a key and calmly unlocked the door of the forbidden laboratory. For one whose heart was wounded by the "things of death," he had a casual way about him with his master's inner sanctum.

It was casual of him, too, to leave the door ajar as he stepped through. His move left me, of course, in almost total darkness. Only a dim night radiance filtered from the distant windows as I crept silently after him toward the casket. And once again, I had barely time to flatten myself against the wall when, without warning, my quarry emerged from the room, light pointing floorward, and swept past me less than two feet from my face. Taut with purpose, yet graceful and silent as ever, he followed his dwindling light back along the way that we had come.

It was unthinkable, I told myself, that he had accomplished his mission. No one in his right mind would prowl the house at two in the morning simply to unlock a door and leave it open. I racked my brain for an explanation and decided that he had retraced his steps for something left behind—something that I felt sure he would bring back.

Meanwhile, I had my chance. The nosiness of Bluebeard's wife was on me. I had to see what was inside the room—I simply *had* to know what secret of the laboratory drew the Parsi butler from his bed.

The room held a pitchy, palpable darkness. Moving forward with the greatest caution over a tilelike floor, I stumbled against a shin-bruising device that seemed to be made of metal and porcelain. Or so it felt to my groping hands as they described its considerable length and curious detail. I decided that it was, of all things, a barber's chair, and I barely suppressed a spasm of giggles.

Arms out before me, I circled this incongruity, traversed some feet of chilly flooring, and fetched up against a window. The recessed panes felt like glass, but not the barest twinkle of night sky was visible. On either side of the window, the walls appeared to be sheathed in sheet metal. Reaching upward, I could touch my fingers to a low metallic ceiling.

I groped around a corner and glued myself to the side wall. Though I had no real plan of action, it certainly wouldn't do to stand opposite the door—and in the path of an entering flashlight—if and when Jamshid returned.

Return he did. Almost as I took my station, a glow appeared in the hall, and a yellow circle of light shone on the laboratory floor. From the color of the gleam, I judged that his battery was running low.

This time Jamshid shut the door silently behind him. His tall form faintly outlined by the light, he made for the center of the room, stooped down, and deposited something on the floor. There was a sound of metal against tile—almost as if he had set down a heavy frying pan in a bathtub. The frying-pan motif was heightened as he snapped out his light and, in the inky darkness, proceeded to strike sparks, clashing together some sort of rasping instruments.

"The Camp Fire Boys in the Parlor," I thought to myself.

And sure enough, his form took shape again in silhouette as a small white flame writhed upward from in front of him. As he tended the fire, bending low above it, another wisp began its upward dance—and still another.

There is always something magical about the small start of a blaze, and for a moment I was fascinated by the sinuous movement of both man and flame. Frantic indecision rescued me from my trance. It was obvious that, to put it mildly, something had better be done—and I had not the faintest idea what.

I once heard of an Arab prince who visited Paris with his suite and allowed the members of the entourage to roast sacrificial mutton on an Aubusson carpet at the George V. But you don't, as a rule, let even Persian butlers broil their breakfast on the living-room floor; and though the flames were not rising very high, there seemed to be every indication that Jamshid was a pyromaniac. The fact also occurred to me that he was somewhat bigger than I.

He got up just then, and I thought he was coming straight for my corner. Instead, he moved toward the far side of the room. At first his campfire had made our surroundings recede into deeper darkness, but now I had my first glimpse of a wall: dimly and fitfully, it glowed like a metallic barrier, decorated all over with moldings and bosses. Slowly, Jamshid reached out toward it, arms black against the faint reflection, hands grasping at what I realized was a bank of huge and horizontal drawers.

With the slow and solemn movements of a priest, the Parsi pulled one of the drawers part way out from the wall. Behind him in the center of the room, the fire danced and hovered, rising at times as much as two feet from the floor. The drawer moved noiselessly, and Jamshid looked at length upon its content.

Then, with his hands clasped high above his head, he began what I can only suppose was a dirge—a low, guttural chant, at once mournful and angry. Leaving the drawer as it protruded, he returned to his fire, sat himself cross-legged behind it (with his back to me), and continued the plainsong quarter tones of his devotion.

Devotion I knew it to be, and I had no further fear that he was going to great trouble to set the house afire. The apparatus before him, the primitive method of igniting his blaze, the chant—and, above all, the open drawerlike section of the wall—these each had meaning for the Parsi, and each formed part of a solemn ceremonial. As the weird wooing of his song went on, I began to feel that *I* was the intruder—that he was where he had a right to be and I was not.

I must have shifted from one foot to the other or in some way have changed my position, for in the moment that I recognized his work as worship, he saw me reflected in the firelit metal of the farther wall. My only warning was the sharp cessation of his dirge, a sudden stiffening of his figure by the fire—then he was on me.

Mind you, I was almost directly behind him. But he did not bother to turn around. Instead, from where he sat, he launched himself in an incredible back handspring, bringing his feet down like two hammers on my head and shoulder. I crumpled under him, trying to shout, "Lay off, you fool!" But his steely arm was across my face, and as we rolled together on the tiles, his legs clamped around my belly in a killing figure four.

I am not unused to mat encounters from a fair start or a referee's position, but I had never before been struck by the weight of a human body hurled at me horizontally, feet first. That impact in itself was enough for most of me. A crack of my head against the wall and the merciless application of his scissors took care of the rest.

Chapter

10

I have no idea how long I was out. Nor, for the moment, did I know what waked me. Then a touch on my ankle made me stiffen, and a pain shot through my head that almost sent me back to dreamland.

Another stealthy but palpable touching of my ankle. I wondered whether there were mice in the room. But now what I felt were fingers, fingers fooling with my socks. Only I had no socks.

The recollection of combat returned. Was I still in the room with the metal drawers and the indoor grill? I tried to speak, but something dry and chewy had been stuffed into my mouth.

"Sh," said a voice (if you can *say* "sh").

Further manipulation of my feet followed. I moved my hands and felt cold metal. I was lying propped up, apparently, on some kind of articulated table. The barber chair, I thought. Razors any minute. I fingered the stuff in my mouth; it was taped in.

"Sh," said the voice in the dark.

A lightweight object was laid on my stomach. Something reached under me and scratched my back. I heard a curious, shuffling noise like the movement of a big animal. A brief change came over the quality of the darkness—one might say that, for an instant, it thinned. Then, with the least of snicks, the door into the hall was closed, and I knew that I was once more alone in the laboratory of Dr. Sarx.

I started to work on the gag again. (For some reason, it galls me more to have my mouth tied shut than any other part of me restrained.) The weight rolled off my stomach and fell to the floor with a clatter. Tearing the last strip of adhesive from my face, I swung myself up and steadied for a moment on the edge of my couch. The thing was high, for I could barely reach the floor with my toes.

My head began to throb, but I managed to grope about on the tiles till my hand encountered a metal cylinder. From the sound of its falling, I had entertained just a faint, fond hope that it might be what it was—a flashlight. (Though whether Jamshid's or another, I had no idea; nor any as to why some other prowling denizen of Sexton's Prim should so provide me.)

It was not Jamshid's—unless he had replaced his battery, for now a bright beam beat on the strange articulated table and the wall of drawers—with every panel smoothly shut— and on the center of the white-tiled floor where a faint ring of darkness was the only trace of Jamshid's furtive barbecue. Under the table-couch lay a strip of rumpled cloth, which I guessed had recently been tied about my ankles. For no particular reason, I picked it up.

Warily, I made my way to the door but switched off my light before I reached it. In the hall a dim bulb burned where none had been before. Out of the corner of my eye, I saw that the *kilim* had slipped clean off the casket. My head felt better, and I wondered whether I should wake someone to report my tale of terror. Charlie was my only inspiration, and—except that it was somewhere at the back—I wasn't even sure where he slept. I had left my watch under my pillow and had no idea what time it was, but as I stood outside the living room in indecision, a yellow warbler started warbling. Something crackly stuck to the back of my pajamas, and I pulled away a piece of paper. In the half light of the hall, I read it, neatly printed:

FOR PETE'S SAKE GO TO BED AND STAY THERE

I did as I was told.

Chapter

11

Dr. Sarx finished his orange juice with a doglike gulp.

"The *ushabti*," he announced. "The *ushabti*—or, as it was originally called, the *shawabti*—is characteristic of the Middle Kingdom." (Indeed yes, I thought. Just the stuff for the morning after.) "Most of them were made of wood," he went on, "but more elegant decedents made arrangements—'preplanning,' we call it—for bronze or faïence or even richer materials."

"But they weren't mummies?" Mrs. Budding's voice, like her face, appeared tired. It was rather obvious that she was making breakfast conversation. "They weren't the—er—the people themselves?"

"Indeed no. Indeed no. The *ushabti* was never used as a container. He was the—what shall I say?—the alter ego of the deceased. It was he who ran the errands and performed the tasks assigned to the departed. For the ancient Egyptian, there was no physical connection between mummy and *ushabti*, no —er—identification in a real sense. Perhaps"—he cocked an eyebrow and looked coyly around the table—"perhaps that was their mistake, eh? What? The failure to identify? Ah well, no matter." He challenged us to disagree with a sweeping pull at the wide mustache.

"The loved one, you understand, remained well fed and undisturbed while this double, the messenger, tended the boat of the gods, tilled the gardens of Paradise, and rode with Re around the heavens." The doctor paused on a mouthful of blood pudding. "Only at night, of course," he added, "only at night. Throughout the day the substitute kept his place—as quiet as Bastet over there." He pointed at one of his own productions, a half-cat figure in pink limestone standing against the wall. He laughed shortly. "One might almost suppose from what you tell me that a *ushabti* was abroad last night."

You don't know the half of it, I thought, having had no opportunity as yet to divulge my late adventures.

For the matter of that, the doctor had received the report of the terrace attack with more of surprise than concern. "Indeed? Indeed! I had no knowledge of these village entanglements. Butrus and Ali are both good boys—simple-minded, loyal *fellahin* really. I shall speak to them seriously."

Lucy's near-accident left him equally unmoved. "A dreadful thing," he said—but I didn't think he thought so— "a dreadful thing. Vickers must check the brakes. Again—yes, thoroughly."

Through all this, Jamshid, my friend of the moonlight hours, walked silently around the table, helping Mrs. B. to scrambled eggs and Dr. Sarx to a second of fried potatoes. (Whatever else you might say about them, these people ate well.) The children, apparently, had breakfasted earlier: I had checked their rooms on my way down and found them empty. Of Ali and Butrus, there was no sound nor sight.

"The canopic jar," said Dr. Sarx, "is a very different thing, a very different thing indeed. *There's* a receptacle, if you like. For the intestines, of course." He speared more of the pudding. "Removed from the side and the incision marked or sealed with an *uza*—a kind of cartouche, you know. Strange that the jar was never a full statuette. Heads for lids, of course

69

—that sort of thing. But never a full statuette. You know, my boy"—he turned to me—"they were doubtless on the verge of something—something greater than man has since dreamed of. But I don't believe they knew it.

"For that matter"—his manner changed—"I hope you had a comfortable night—after the incident of Butrus?"

"The night was very quiet," I assured him, stealing a look at Jamshid. With that gentleman I wanted some long and serious conversation, for I had come to the conclusion that Jamshid had not known who I was when he attacked so suddenly. Not that I thought he would have welcomed my presence at his fireside, but I believed that his protest might have taken a different form. The truth of the matter was—as I learned to my surprise—that he thought that in our tussle I had not recognized *him*.

I cornered him in the library after breakfast, and he tried to play the innocent.

"The *âghâ* has dreamt this thing of fighting and of the laboratory. Is the *âghâ* not aware that I am forbidden to approach the furniture of death? Was the *âghâ* not told last night that I myself have no key to the chamber?"

I thought he was going to quote Scripture—"Dost thou not know? Hast thou not heard?"—and all the time his great brown eyes were on me, filled with Iranian righteousness. There was remarkable compulsion in his gaze. If I had let him speak on without stopping, he might well have convinced me of almost anything—that I hadn't followed him from the upstairs hall or spied on his doings in the room of drawers or wrestled with him in a dying firelight across a tile-hard floor. Of what had happened after I lost consciousness, I could not directly accuse him, but certainly I was entitled to suspicion.

"Jamshid," I said, "if I had any sense, the police would be here in the house this minute." Indeed, although I didn't tell him so, he had only my bewilderment to thank for the fact that I hadn't reported to anyone: so many queer things had happened that I scarcely trusted myself.

"You know perfectly well," I told him, "that you were up in the children's hallway last night and that you let yourself into the laboratory with a key. You came out and then returned—with some sort of Sterno outfit. You opened one of the drawers in the wall, caught a glimpse of my reflection, and nailed me with a perfectly wonderful back flip. Then you mashed my gizzard with a figure four till the lights went out.

"What you did after that, you know better than I do." I could not go into the details of my awakening, partly because the experience itself had been hazy and more especially because I wasn't sure that it had been Jamshid who released me. The absurd placard on the back of my pajamas hardly seemed in Oriental taste.

He heard my accusation without the least change of expression. Finally, he shook his head.

"Dreams, *âghâ*, dreams arising out of the accident to my friend Butrus."

"Dreams, my foot," I said. "I didn't dream a sore belly, and I didn't dream you tied me up with this."

I whipped from my pocket the strip of white cloth that I had picked up from the laboratory floor. It was precisely the stuff of which his long white coats were made: it might have been torn from the very garment he was wearing.

At once his manner altered. He smiled as if amused, but there was a new edge to his voice.

"You recall also how you escaped from this bond?" He sounded as if he really wanted to know, and I felt surer than ever that my escape had surprised him.

"What I recall," I said, "has nothing to do with it. I should like some sort of explanation of your behavior, and if I don't get it, I shall go to Dr. Sarx with the whole crazy tale."

"*You* will go to the *tashrif?* You who have been here for two days—with a story to tell of me?—of one who has served this house for years?" He laughed pleasantly. "My dear Mr. Flower! How if it were *I* who was wakened last night by *your* illicit wanderings? How if I saw you enter the room which is forbidden—into which it is well known that I never enter? How if I have held my peace till now out of mere pity for your adolescent indiscretion? Is there any to support your untried word against mine?"

I didn't care much for that "adolescent indiscretion" stuff, but I saw his point.

"Except for the fantasy of combat," he went on, "you suffered nothing in this dream. Nor do you say that you saw anything of evil done. You have not told me your dream of returning to your room, but it is my advice, *âghâ,* that you keep all your dreams to yourself." (At the start of our interview, I had scarcely expected a lecture, but I was surely getting one.) "There is enough of evil in this house for both of us. I have my sphere and you have yours. Even now, *âghâ,* I do not believe that you know where your charges are."

Like a well-rehearsed performer, exactly on cue, Lucy came into the room.

"Where's Warburton, Posy?" she asked. "I haven't seen him all morning."

Chapter
12

The plain fact was that Warburton was missing. And I don't mean merely unavailable for French, although that, of course, was what we thought at first.

Irritated rather than satisfied by my talk with Jamshid, I decided before anything else to hunt the truant pupil and get on with lessons.

Warburton, it seemed, had not had breakfast with Lucy. She herself had been down early—*"très de bonne heure,"* she told me. And as we kept up our practice of Gallic, she contributed a rather surprising facility to our conversation.

While we checked the house and garage, I inquired as to how polylingual she might be; and she told me a tale of peripatetic childhood, supervised by a variety of *gouvernantes.* The late Mr. Budding, I gathered, had been an Egyptologist by trade. From her sketchy memoir, I tried to form an idea of the man: the proverbial dreamy scholar emerged—indifferent to circumstance, dedicated to his profession, yet possessed of a remarkable ability to win affection. Not that Lucy was unduly sentimental about him: you just could tell that he had been a hard man to lose.

His twin children had been born in a Middle Kingdom storehouse at El-Kob, and Lucy's earliest memories were of a dig at Kom-Ombo where the temple of Sobek was—as she put it—"*étouffé de crocodiles.*" Intermittent journeys had taken the family to other lands, classical mainly—with a year in Athens and two or three summers in Alexandria. For a time Mr. B. had been a cultural attaché in Tehran, and there the little Buddings had picked up a smatter of Iranian, while their parents acquired the redoubtable Jamshid. (I was somewhat surprised to learn that my athletic buddy was of *their* camp, for I had assumed that he belonged to Dr. Sarx's collection.)

The whole story reminded me somewhat of my own childhood, largely spent in travel with my father—until I was old enough for the several boarding schools at which his profession and his widowerhood had forced him to park me. But where I had no memories at all of my mother, Lucy remembered vividly her father's falling ill in Medinet Habu, his search for a cure in the West, and his final acceptance of an invitation from Caspar Sarx (an amateur of archaeology himself) for a visit meant to be a convalescence. The convalescence part had not worked out. At Sexton's Prim, it appeared, Mr. Budding had died—something over a year ago. Naturally, I didn't press Lucy for details.

"Cutty claims he's some kind of uncle of Munce's," Lucy explained. "That's why we've stayed, and that's why Munce does his letters for him." Unless Warren Budding had saved more than most Egyptologists, it was easy to understand how the young widow had chosen to remain with her twins under the protection of her husband's friend.

Lucy grunted, biting the back of her thumb and lapsing into English. "I guess that's why she lets him carve her every day."

We were standing in the downstairs hall, not far from the laboratory door. I observed that last night's casket had not yet been removed but was neatly swathed in its protective *kilim.*

Lucy seemed to notice nothing unusual, and I decided that her brother was a safer subject.

"Maybe Warburton's in on the carving," I suggested.

"Maybe. But I doubt it. We might stop in and see."

"Dr. Sarx won't mind?"

"No. He's fairly all right about the studio. It's the lab that's forbidden fruit. Nobody gets in *there*—except Butrus and Ali, that is." She hesitated, then asked me: "By the way, have you seen the Gnome?"

"The what?"

"The Gnome—you know—a little man with whiskers. He's been around since early this morning. I'll bet he's the one that gave Ali the bumps."

"Now wait a minute," I said. "Are you talking about somebody on the place?" I meant someone in Dr. Sarx's employ, but she took me literally.

"He was on the place ten minutes ago right back of the garage." We had come around the house that way. "I didn't *think* you saw him. A kind of hunchback, bent-over little man with a brown beard and dark glasses. I saw him early this morning. I went to wake Warburton, but Warburton wasn't in his room, and by the time I got back, he was gone—the Gnome, I mean. Warburton must have gotten up ahead of the birds." She sounded indignant.

"Where did you see this—Gnome?" I asked.

"Out of my window. He was standing on the terrace outside the lab, smoking a pipe. And just now—just as we got to the front of the garage, he ducked behind it. Are you sure you're not pretending you didn't see him?"

I wasn't sure who was pretending what, but Lucy's story had the ring of truth about it. I wondered how long a time had elapsed between my final going to bed and her phenomenally early rising. I wondered, too, whether my employer had brought the Gnome back with him. Or had the

Gnome something to do with my rescue from the laboratory?

"Do you suppose your friend arrived with Dr. Sarx?" I asked her.

"Oh, no. I'd gone down to the beach and back before Cutty drove in." She looked at me curiously. "You must have slept like a rock," she said.

I must confess that as a baby-sitter I felt somewhat deflated. The junior Buddings were obviously independent souls, and I had noticed no great anxiety on their mother's part as to where they were or what they did. Nor had I been given any real instructions as to their care and feeding—except the suggestion about French. As far as I could see, I had been hired to keep the twins in a general way out of their uncle's hair. If Warburton was visiting the studio, it probably behooved me to remove him.

"Come on," I said. "Lead me to the carving chamber."

Obviously built, as I had guessed, in very recent years, it turned out to be an amazing room. Connected by a lengthy breezeway to the house, its brick exterior and huge north light contrasted oddly with the traditional New England aspect of the larger building.

There was just one room inside, but the spacious floor was cluttered with a wild profusion of artistic jetsam. Stone slabs, granite fragments, odd chunks of schist, paintpots, dropcloths, chisels, and mallets crowded each other for space. A drawing board on horses was backed uselessly into a corner; huge canvas sheets here and there covered vague bulky figures; and through the welter of debris, one could make out a number of enormous chests, standing against two of the four walls. (I took them—correctly, as it turned out—for the superstructure of *mastabas,* benchlike covers of ancient tombs.) Only in front of the great window was a space cleared, perhaps twelve feet square.

In the center of this clearing, Dr. Sarx, in Oriental gown, worked in some sort of stony plastic on the almost finished, more than life-sized, likeness of his model. Mrs. Budding herself, dressed as she had been on the previous morning, sat quietly on what appeared to be a granite tree stump. She was reading a magazine.

Neither of them paid us any attention as we entered by a metal door at the end of the studio. Mrs. Budding was absorbed, and the doctor appeared rapt—completely fascinated by his work, his hands alive with quick and graceful gestures, but his eyes—insofar as I could see through the various obstructions—implacably fixed on his model.

Lucy had seen this sort of thing before and was unawed by the spectacle of concentration.

"Excuse me," she said, "but has anybody seen Warburton?"

Neither Mrs. Budding nor the doctor answered.

"Has anybody seen Warburton? He seems to have skipped breakfast."

Mrs. Budding turned languidly on her tree trunk. "It wouldn't be the first time, Lucy dear. Perhaps he's gone to the post office with Vickers."

"Of course!" There was annoyance in the doctor's tone. "Now if we may have that profile again, my dear—"

"I wish he wouldn't call her that." We were outside once more, and Lucy sighed her wish. "It sounds so sort of—what's the word, Posy?—as if he owned her or something!"

"Proprietary," I suggested. "Yes, I get what you mean. I'm impressed with his sculpture, though. For the rough sort of stuff he's working in, that's a remarkable job he's done on your mother. Does he make everything so big—on so large a scale?"

" 'A third larger than life,' " Lucy told me—she was quoting. "That's his motto. You ought to see *me*—and Warburton."

I was lost for a moment, but she explained. "We're both done—finished—even painted. 'A third larger than life.' We look like a couple of overgrown *ushabtis,* and I s'pose that's what we are. But I haven't noticed that the figures run any errands for us. Maybe we have to be dead before they start working." She was silent for just a fraction of a minute. Then: "We're in there," she said, and jerked a thumb back toward the studio.

"I didn't see you."

"We're under canvas—to keep us from fading, he says. We're over in the far corner. Eventually, we're going to be shown—when he gets Munce done. There's something special about a family group, apparently. Nothing like it has been seen since the Middle Kingdom. Warburton's been inside his."

"Inside?"

"The statues open up, you know. Their backs are hinged somehow. Warburton dared me to get into mine, but I wouldn't. Not after the accident, anyway."

"What accident?" I asked.

She looked uncomfortable. "Oh, it was nothing. Nothing on purpose, at least. But the whole thing gives me the willies. Warburton says it's just 'the whim of one obsessed.' Warburton puts things well. Don't you think so?"

"Yes, he does," I admitted. "And what *about* Warburton?"

"Oh," she said. "I forgot. But I don't believe he went to the post office. I bet I know where he went. I bet he's fishing. Last thing last night, he said he wanted to think; and whenever Warburton wants to think, he goes fishing."

I offered something about going to look for Charlie Vickers, but she pooh-poohed me.

"I'll talk French," she promised. "Come on. Let's go to the beach. Maybe he's down there talking to Mr. Snow."

"Since dawn?" I asked.

"It could be. Or they may both have gone out for eel. Warburton *loves* eel."

So did—so *do*—I, and I allowed myself to be drawn along. *"Matelote d'anguille bourguignonne,"* I murmured to myself.

78

Chapter

13

Mr. Snow was not at his shanty. The back door, under the lobster sign, was locked. The sliding front doors were apparently barred on the inside.

"I wonder whether the pram's in there. It's usually on the beach," Lucy said, "unless Warburton's taken it. And he'd only do that to reach *Bluejacket*."

But *Bluejacket* was firmly moored some hundred yards offshore and bobbed on a short line in the morning chop. The sun was bright on the water, but Gannet Bay was empty of boats. Between our shore and the opposite island, whitecaps broke the blue—like feathers.

"Does anyone live over there?" I asked.

"On the island? There used to. But the place has been closed the last two summers." She told me that a large house lay back of the distant dunes, its anchorage beyond the island. "They had a thirty-six-foot cruiser—very swish."

"What about your uncle's—Dr. Sarx's—*Queen of Sheba*? She sounds pretty swish, too. Does he often use her?"

Lucy sighed. "Not nearly so often as we wish he would. Once in a while he takes a long trip on her—two or three days away. But he doesn't take any of us—except last time he took Ali. Ali and Butrus came that way, you know."

"Indeed? Where from?"

"Oh, we asked Cutty, and he more or less told us to mind our own business. But I don't think he caught them in the ocean, do you?"

She looked past me, gazing up the line of shore that fronted what I took to be the Little property. Up to this point, I had not thought that she was particularly concerned about her brother; but now, suddenly, she seemed restless and dissatisfied.

"Tell you what," she said, "maybe he's looking for scallop seeds. They grow on the back of the water grass—little black things, you know. You can tell what kind of scallop year it's going to be by the number of babies. The pram would be just right for nudging into shallows. You go that way"—she pointed northward—"and I'll walk down past the guns."

The water slapped against the shore, and miniature breakers rolled up close to our feet. Lucy waved and went her way.

I wandered in the opposite direction, looking for footprints or traces of the pram. Beyond me at some distance, the stream that ran through the Littles' place debouched into the bay. There the reeds grew tall, and I told myself that it would be impossible to see a small boat—or a small boy—without entering the brook itself. To do so, I decided, would be easier by water than by land. Accordingly, I shed my tennis shoes, leaving them on the beach, and waded out to where the grass grew down into the wavelets. The water was clear, and I saw the fiddler crabs again and hoped they would not take my toes for a sonata; but they were following a school of baby mummichog and paid me no attention.

I had paddled my way past half the reedy point when something made me stop and listen. Except for the gentle splashing of my feet and the hum of the wind on the waves, there had been no sound. And then I heard it—from somewhere up the little creek beyond me—a human voice, thin, strained, and wispy, upraised in song.

I knew at once that it could not be Warburton: the tones were cracked and more than middle-aged, the faintly wind-borne melody was a quaint old-fashioned air, and the words were as yet quite indistinguishable. Stepping inshore, I parted the reeds and moved in the direction of the creek. But the green blades grew thick from the sand, and it was several minutes before I stood on the edge of the rivulet.

It was scarcely more than that—a shallow channel some six feet across, dug by the water's action so the brook could meet the bay. For some distance the stream ran straight to my right, then curved away to flow unseen behind the upper reeds.

The eerie song grew louder, and I caught a word or two. Then from around the bend, there came in sight the bow of what appeared to be a duckboat, gray and flat and—at first glance—empty. Indeed, the queer craft seemed to be self-propelled until I saw a hand and arm that trailed across the gunwale to make vague and finny gestures in the water.

Slowly, the duckboat came nearer, borne on the gentle current of the creek; and word by word the antic song grew more distinct:

> " 'How should I your truelove know
>   From another one?
>   By his cockle hat and staff—' "

The verse was interrupted by what sounded like a sneeze.

> " 'He is dead and gone, lady,
>   He is dead and gone. . . .
>   Tomorrow is Saint Valentine's day—' "

In the shallow bottom of the undecked boat, stretched at full length on her back, lay Chicken Little's grandmother. She was swathed, as I had seen her before, in filmy draperies, and these garments were festooned with ropes of seaweed. Queenly oblivious to all besides herself, she caroled as she came:

> " *'White his shroud as mountain snow—*
>   *Larded with sweet flowers. . . .'* "

She trailed her hand in the water, and her duckboat came to a stop almost directly at my feet. Her eyes were closed, but from somewhere beneath her, she produced a folded piece of paper. This, with an upthrust, bony arm, she proffered me, and since it was within my reach, I grabbed for it.

" 'There's rue for you,' " she said. " 'Oh, you must wear your rue with a difference.' "

The spit of sand on which I stood was soft and shifting, and reaching for her gift, I very nearly lost my balance. Her eyes opened for a second; then with a sudden surge of motion, she half sat, backwatered vigorously once, and resumed her supine posture.

The duckboat moved away, its pointed stern serving as well for a bow. Mrs. Little had arrived head-first; now her feet led her back upstream. And from the homebound barge, there came, *diminuendo,* further portions of Ophelia's song:

> " *'They bore him barefaced on the bier,*
>   *Hey non nonny, nonny, hey nonny,*
>   *And in his grave rained many a tear—*
>   *Fare you well, my dove!'* "

Wordless I was indeed. Nor shall I apologize. I suppose that I should have greeted my apparition politely: "Good morning, Mrs. Little. A pleasant trip, I hope?"—or something like that. Truth to tell, I simply had not the stuff; for three or four minutes after she had vanished around the bend, I stood like an idiot, the prisoner of astonishment, clasping a silly fold of paper.

Which same paper made no impression upon me at all until

I had stepped down into the shallow stream, skirted the thrust of shoreline reeds, and regained the bit of beach where I had left my tennis shoes. Only then, when it got in my way, did I think to open the lady's letter. It was printed in squarish capitals and minced no words. What I read was this:

STICK WITH THE KID, YOU ASS

I thought perhaps I'd better and hurried back to find Lucy.

"There isn't a sign of him," she told me, "but I saw the Gnome." Lucy was sitting on one of the old rails in front of Mr. Snow's shanty. Sounds from within the silvery shack suggested that its owner had returned.

"Yes," said Lucy, answering my look. "Mr. Snow's in there. I told him all about it—about Warburton and the pram and the Gnome, too. You didn't have any luck, did you?"

On an impulse, I reported the strange encounter with Mrs. Little. I expected astonishment, but Lucy showed none.

"That's nothing," she said. "She floats around like that all the time. That duckboat's her pride and joy. She had the cockpit taken out so she could lie down in the thing. She's even been out in the bay with it. Some days she reads, but most of the time she simply sings. On land, you know, she runs a shandrydan."

"A *what?*"

"A shandrydan, a juice buggy—you know, a car with batteries."

Most cars had batteries, I thought, but I didn't argue the point.

Lucy paused, then added, "She never wrote that letter."

With some misgiving, I had shown her the printed message.

"How do you know?" I asked.

"Because she doesn't talk that way. She'd say it in poetry or something—'Guard well the little maiden'—that's Grandma's style. In fact"—Lucy spoke thoughtfully—"in fact, I don't know anybody around here who would write that way—to you. Unless—"

"Unless what?"

"Oh, nothing," she said. Then, uncomfortably: "I get silly ideas sometimes."

"Tell me about the Gnome," I suggested. "Where did you see him?"

"Up in the bushes back of the battery." She was talking, of course, about the two six-pounders. "He didn't see me because I was close up under the dunes. He's not so gnomish as I thought. But he wears short trousers—not shorts, you know, but those things that fold over your knee socks—like golfers in the olden days. Remember?"

I remembered Walter Hagen, and I was increasingly intrigued by Lucy's friend. A short pipe-smoker in plus fours who kept bird-watcher's hours—I liked the sound of him. It's always more fun when the wicked are picturesque.

"Did you ask Mr. Snow's opinion about Warburton? About what we ought to do?" I could fairly *see* the line in some book on psychology: "In time of stress youth turns inevitably and gladly to age." I wasn't particularly glad about it, but I surely felt that I could use some counsel. And so I asked my question rather loudly—and Mr. Snow answered for himself.

"Don't know what to make of it, Posy. Wabbit'n wouldn't take the pram past the moorin's. But the pram's gone and Wabbit'n's gone. Must be some connection. 'Less, of course, somebody took the pram and Wabbit'n went for a walk."

I couldn't tell whether Mr. Snow was being funny or covering up a real concern. I myself was becoming acutely conscious of my shortcomings as a boy-sitter.

"I'd better say something to Mrs. Budding," I said. "She knows we started to look for him."

"Munce is going to lunch with Torky Torquil," Lucy informed us. "She has my approval. You and I'll probably have to have lunch alone."

"What about the doctor?" I asked.

"He usually works right through— when he's had a sitting, I mean. They take him a sandwich or something to the studio, but half the time he doesn't touch it. After all, he does pretty well at breakfast."

"It just may be," Mr. Snow broke in, "that 'twere better not to say anything about Wabbit'n till we've had a little more time. I'm going over to the island 'bout an hour from now. Can't believe the boy'd take the pram over there, but I can nose around. Got some pots to lift t'other side. Better wait a bit, I think, 'fore you get folks worried."

The bright blue eyes in the brown face seemed to twinkle with sincerity and concern. It was inconceivable that this sturdy old salt could be less than straightforward. And yet his advice bothered me. Hadn't it been Mr. Snow who was concerned over the safety chain? Wasn't he the one to see considerably more than playful malice in the sabotage of *Bluejacket*? Vague as my orders were, Warburton represented 50 whole per cent of my responsibility. I felt that someone ought to know—that someone ought to be told—and as soon as possible.

I looked at Mr. Snow again, and he nodded in what I supposed was reassurance. " 'Twon't do to worry ahead of time, son. Wabbit'n's bound to turn up."

But it didn't convince me. In fact, it seemed almost out of character. The Cape Codders I had known had always been superfearful for their summer people—overly anxious about their inept seamanship, pitying and yet protective. Mr. Snow's quiet confidence—especially in one of Warburton's tender years—actually quickened my suspicions.

On our way back to the house, I asked Lucy what she thought. I had come to have considerable respect for the young lady's judgment. Did she think Mr. Snow was to be trusted?

She did—to the uttermost, apparently.

"He knows something," she said.

I found small comfort in the possibility but didn't say so. Something else was on my mind: "Is it hard to get into this place at night?" I asked.

"There's the telephone at the gate," she told me; and I remembered that on the night of my arrival, Charlie Vickers had mentioned such an instrument. "You have to have a key to use it," she went on, "and anybody who comes in late is supposed to call the house. But you can't *make* 'em. And there's just the low wall along one side—down by the road—and the bay along the other, of course, but nothing else to stop anybody. After all, we run for nearly half a mile along the shore. Are you thinking of the man who bongoed Butrus?"

I was impressed. "Not particularly," I said. Sexton's Prim must be one of the few really big places remaining on the crowded Cape.

As we neared the garage, Torquil's Bugatti rounded the drive and slowed at sight of us. From the seat beside the driver, Mrs. Budding spoke to Lucy.

"I'm going to lunch with Mr. Torquil," she said. Not a word or question about Warburton!

"I know," said Lucy. "You told us."

"Oh did I? I suppose I did—"

"Mrs. Budding," I cut in, but she paid me no attention.

"Oh—and, Lucy, that reminds me," she said. "I'm worried about your uncle. Wait a minute, Fran." Mr. Torquil had started to roll slowly forward. "Let me tell Lucy. There was a letter brought your uncle while I was still sitting—and I thought he was going to have a stroke. I've never seen him so upset. He stopped work and practically ordered me to go and change. Then he shut himself into the study, and he's been there ever since."

"Who brought the letter?" I asked.

"Who what—? Oh, Jamshid brought the letter. It had no stamp on it. I really thought Uncle Caspar would faint. I doubt if he'll be at lunch, dear."

Without a further word, she waved her driver on, and the Bugatti moved away with a pleasant snort of power.

"Well," Lucy commented. "You didn't have much chance, did you?"

She was right. I hadn't had much chance to speak of Warburton and ease my conscience. But Lucy's mind, apparently, was on the road with her mother.

"He's a pretty constructive guy," she remarked. "Torky, I mean. He's renting a place beyond the Littles'. Nobody knows what he does. Old Mrs. Little likes him, treats him like a favorite nephew. Maybe they're related. Warburton says he's a spy for our side—America's James Bond, or something. Warburton likes James Bond."

This assortment of information did nothing either for my morale or for my appetite. Lunch, as predicted, was a twosome, but I took small pleasure in the plaice *amandine*. Jamshid was serving us some very good water ice (not sherbet, thank you!) when I got up my courage to ask him a question.

"Warburton hasn't been back?—back here at the house?"

With typical indirection he replied, "I have not seen him, *âghâ*."

"Oh," I said fatuously. Then, as an afterthought: "I hear Dr. Sarx got a letter. Er—Mrs. Budding told us he seemed upset."

Jamshid inclined his head in silence. He might as well have come right out with it and said, "What earthly business is it of yours?" But he didn't, and I went brashly on.

"I understand it wasn't stamped. Where can it have come

from?" (Considering the fact that I knew Jamshid had delivered it, this was carrying *naïveté* pretty far.)

Surprisingly, the Parsi butler made no protest. "The letter was handed to me this morning in the village, *âghâ*. It was addressed to the *tashrif,* and I was asked to give it to him in person. Naturally, I had no notion of its contents nor of the fact that it might prove distressing. Nor had I ever before seen the man who asked of me this favor."

And he tipped you well, I thought. Aloud I asked, "What did he look like?"

"He was a slight man, *âghâ,* with a short brown beard. His eyes were shaded, and he wore, as it were, Turkish trousers."

"The Gnome!" breathed Lucy. Jamshid looked a little startled.

"And you have no idea what the message was?" My question, I knew, crossed the borders of rudeness. A spasm of indignation tinged the handsome, swarthy face.

"How could I possibly know, *âghâ?* The *tashrif* did not read it aloud. Nor did he ask me how I came by it."

I caught the rebuke but said nothing. Jamshid remained by the table as if waiting for a further order. Finally he said, "I, too, have a question, *âghâ.* The boy—he is with Mr. Snow?"

He seemed to wait with eagerness on my reply.

"No," I said. "No. Mr. Snow hadn't seen him."

Jamshid's eyes looked frightened as he cleared away our places. As soon as he had left the room, I told Lucy of my resolve.

"I don't care what Mr. Snow may think," I said. "I'm not going to keep this business of your brother to myself. You haven't seen him since last night; and as far as I can make out, nobody's seen him this morning. Your mother didn't seem particularly interested, and I have reasons of my own for not confiding in Jamshid. You seem to share the general opinion that little boys can disappear at will and no harm done. Well, I *don't* share it. I'm going straight to Dr. Sarx—upset though he may be—and I'm going to tell him that Warburton's disappeared."

I couldn't decide from her expression whether she favored this outburst or not. She made no immediate comment; then she said, "I'll go with you."

So together we left the dining room, traversed the hall, and stood outside the study door. Its mahogany elegance was firmly closed, and I knocked three times. There was no answer from within, and with the thought that his upset magnificence might be taking a nap, I repeated the signal more loudly.

"He hates to be disturbed," whispered Lucy. I realized suddenly that she was trembling in her boots.

I knocked again.

No answer.

I took the doorknob in hand and rattled it. It turned, but the door was bolted from the inside. There was no keyhole to probe or peek through.

"What do we do now?" I asked—and to myself: Is he apt to sulk in silence? Would he deliberately sit there and say nothing while a couple of suppliants hammered on his portal?

Lucy came up with a sensible proposal. "Let's go around outside," she said, "and talk to him through the window."

Around outside we went, where the leaded panes of a bay casement stood open, curtains fluttering in the breeze.

"Dr. Sarx," I called. I didn't want to shout: this was a private errand.

The curtains fluttered, but there was no sound from within the room.

Chapter 15

"Lift me up and I can crawl through," said Lucy. "There's a window seat just inside."

I did as she suggested and watched her rounded stern disappear into the shadowy study. A moment later she called to me, "He isn't here."

With the room locked tight? This was one for the good John Dickson Carr. Somehow I couldn't imagine the fat doctor making his exit by the window route. There was none too much room for me as I shouldered my way through. But besides ourselves, no one was present. No side doors offered an escape; the walls were broken only by bookshelves from floor to ceiling. Here and there a statuette of schist or diorite broke up the march of books. A basalt cat, bigger than the one in the living room, separated Enoch Siskin on *Embalming* from J. K. Schneppel's *Seventy Days in Natron.*

"There's a real one in there," said Lucy. I must have looked puzzled. "A real cat," she explained, "inside the statuette. He put her in there six months ago. He says she couldn't possibly have suffered. Do you think she did?"

I was trying to absorb this new insight into life at Sexton's Prim when the phone rang on the doctor's desk. We were both startled, but when Lucy looked at me inquiringly, arching her small blonde brows, I shook my head. I felt sure that the call would be answered somewhere in the house. But strangely, the phone kept ringing.

Lucy whispered to me as if the phone could overhear, "It's his private line, from the gate."

Under the most normal circumstances, I know of few things harder to withstand than a nagging telephone. Only dead men or brave souls in bathtubs have the nerve, as a rule, to ignore the tingling summons. My curiosity is as strong as most.

"Hello," I said, lowering my pitch a little. My eye caught the calendar on the desk before me. It was heavily marked. A bright red ring circled the current date.

"Hello—Doctor Sarx?" The accent was coarse, the voice husky and unrecognizable. It could have been a tough with a cold or a gent in disguise.

"Speaking," I said. And so I was.

"You got the message?"

"Yes," I said. (After all, I *had* gotten a message—that very morning.)

"Then listen. The price on the kid is what we wrote—O.K.?" I didn't think the man was asking for permission. He was simply making sure I understood.

I made a bleating noise, which passed, apparently, for assent.

"An' you got the dope about the cops?" It was practically a statement of fact. And what was the point, under these circumstances, of admitting that I was not Dr. Sarx?

"Yes," I said. "I understand."

"You better. Eleven o'clock, then. Onna nose."

"Yes," I said, and then I added a very foolish and unSarxlike thing. "Keep the home fires burning," I said.

The man on the phone neither snarled at me nor hung up. With an oddly weighted stress on the pronoun, he told me, "*You* wait and see."

Then the line went dead.

"I could hear," said Lucy. "It was about Warburton, wasn't it?"

"Perhaps it was," I answered, trying to sound cheerful.

But her voice was very small indeed. "Look what I found. It was in the scrapbasket." She held out a crumpled sheet of yellow tablet paper. This is about him, too."

I spread out the paper on the desk. It was printed in capitals of a kind I had seen before. It read:

> "WE GOT WHAT YOURE LOOKING FOR.
> TEN GRAND ELEVEN OCLOCK TONIGHT AT
> THE GATE ALONE NO COPS OR ELSE."

"You've read it?" She nodded. "Your uncle must have gone for the police." (Why hadn't he phoned for them, I wondered?)

"Not the police," she said. "I bet he's gone to get the money."

"But how did he go? Out the window? And why the locked door?"

"I s'pose he came in here to read the message over and think about it. And he didn't want to be disturbed, so he locked the door. And he wanted people to think he was still here, so he went out the way we came in. He'd have had quite a job getting through that window, wouldn't he?"

She prattled on in an effort, I thought, to keep from thinking about Warburton. My own head was spinning with dreadful possibilities: Warburton in the hands of degenerate gangsters—Warburton tortured—Warburton. . . . I tried to check my imagination, but I have always had a great capacity for suspecting the worst.

There was no possibility of the phone call's being a hoax. The note precluded any such pleasant thought. And the voice on the wire had sounded businesslike and tough—so much so, in fact, as to scare me out of any questions.

But now what was I to do? The doctor had disappeared; I had no idea where Mrs. Budding had gone with Torquil; besides Lucy and me, only Jamshid had any knowledge of the message and its origin. Ought I to take a car and pursue the doctor or—in spite of the enemy's warning, both written and spoken—ought I to call the police?

Some words of my father's came back to me—on the subject of dealing with criminals. "Never make a bargain with them," he had said. "The reason they're criminals is that they don't keep bargains. What they promise isn't worth a groat. The only way to deal with them is through the law."

If he meant the more formal processes of law, he was certainly not speaking for himself: the nature of his State Department job had often, I knew, made him a law unto himself. But the gist of his teaching, applied to my present predicament, spoke very clearly: forget the warnings and call the cops.

Lucy unlatched the study door and opened it. "I'm going to tell Jamshid," she said. "*He*'ll know what to do." She started out into the hall—and I after her.

She was walking quickly toward the rear of the house.

"Lucy Budding"—I spoke in my most commanding tones —"Lucy Budding, you come straight back here and talk to nobody until I tell you to. I'm calling the police."

She turned and came slowly back to me. "It said not to— 'no cops or else,'" she quoted. And the fear that shook her sturdy little person was contagious. I, too, would have liked to talk to someone—but Jamshid! The soreness around my middle brought back strong suspicions of that wily Parsi. The trouble was, I had suspicions all around: the good guys refused to distinguish themselves from the bad ones.

"Uncle Cutty doesn't like the cops," Lucy told me. "The one from the village was over here one day simply to talk to Mrs. Simpson, and Cutty practically threw him off the place."

I remembered our avoidance of constabulary at the time that Butrus was bashed. The more I thought of it, the more contrived seemed Jamshid's pleading at that time—the village enemy and all the rest. Jamshid was out. Lucy might think of him as a tried and trusty friend, but my experience argued otherwise.

"Jamshid doesn't like cops either," I said. "And"—pulling myself together—"I shouldn't be surprised if Dr. Sarx has gone to them already—whether he likes them or not."

She shook her head in stubborn disagreement.

"I'll tell you what I'll do," I promised her. "I'll call the cops and ask whether anybody's phoned—from here, I mean. Then at least we'll know where we stand."

"All right," she said, and we went back into the study.

There was no dial on the phone, but whether it was a private line to the gate or not, I got the operator and asked her for the police. She sounded excited, and I'm sure she stayed on the line.

"Hello?"

"Hello," I said. "This is Mr. Greensleeves, Emmet Greensleeves at Sexton's Prim." (I was glad to hear Lucy giggle.)

"Oh?" The constabulary voice was noncommittal.

"Excuse my bothering you, but have you had a call from here—from Sexton's Prim—Dr. Sarx's place? A trouble call?"

"Trouble? What kind of trouble? If there's something wrong with your phone, call the business office—they'll take care of you."

I sighed. "No, you misunderstand. There's nothing wrong with the phone. I'm simply asking for information."

"Information? All you have to do is ask the operator. She'll give you information."

This was getting silly.

"Look," I said. "This is Emmet Greensleeves. I'm a guest here at Sexton's Prim, and Dr. Sarx asked me to call and inquire as to whether you have had any previous calls from here this afternoon. It seems that someone has been using the phone—"

"To call the police?" Light had dawned. "No, sir. Nobody's called us from there. No calls from your phone."

"Oh. Thank you very much. Good-by."

"You're welcome. 'By now."

When I finally got it, it was the answer I had feared. Sarx had made no report to the police. Or—suddenly I saw that my laborious conversation had proved nothing!—had he called them and sworn them to secrecy, fearing a check by the kidnappers? I weighed the likelihoods. On the whole, I thought it more probable that he was planning to play ball with the Amalekites—and might very well, as Lucy had suggested, be already engaged in raising the requisite cash.

I had felt that in my character of Mr. Greensleeves I might resume the conversation by turning in a genuine alarm. But having said that unauthorized calls were being made, my own authority would be immediately questioned if I reported anything like the real trouble.

The possibility remained of phoning the police again—as myself. But in that case, I should have to explain about Greensleeves. It looked as if I had really laid myself an egg.

Lucy started to fry it. "If you call them again before Cutty comes back, he'll be furious, absolutely furious. And Warburton'll probably get 'or else.' You mustn't do it, Posy, you mustn't!"

I didn't know *what* to do. Maybe Jamshid was a good idea after all. Or Mr. Snow—what about him? He ought to be back soon, perhaps with Warburton in hand—or with news of him at least.

"What about Mr. Snow?" I asked. "Why don't we try him again?"

"But the warnings!" Lucy protested.

"The warnings don't say anything about Mr. Snow. And

there's still a chance that they were faked. Maybe Warburton's—er—lost and somebody knows it, and they're just trying to take advantage of the situation by scaring us all."

"They've done that all right," said Lucy. But she agreed to a last try at the beach.

In the light of later events, I may say that the house, as we left it, seemed totally deserted. No sounds came from the kitchen; the assistants were, as usual, invisible; I was thankful that there was no sign of Jamshid. The doctor, apparently, had taken the Cadillac, and Charlie Vickers was off somewhere in the truck. Only the Corvette stood in the otherwise empty garage.

Unfortunately, the beach was empty, too. No trace of the missing pram; no trace of Warburton; no trace—except that the door of his shanty was unlocked—of Mr. Snow.

Aimlessly, I pushed my way into the crowded workshop. Where the sun slanted through the doorway, I made out a careful confusion of paints, pulleys, nets, gear, and tackle. The smell was delicious. I called out to Lucy, "What kind of tobacco does Mr. Snow smoke?"

From outside she told me, "He doesn't smoke at all."

I had thought not. Yet her answer made me curious, for on the old salt's workbench, propped against a vise, sat a handsome half-filled Dunhill. Even more curious was the fact that when I felt it, the bowl of the pipe was still warm.

I did not mention my find to Lucy as we walked back from the water. We were both depressed. As for Miss Budding, she seemed lost in thought.

I don't know why we stopped at the garage. No siren song was sung to us; no voice invited us to enter; there was no visible enticement. Yet I shall be certain to my dying day that the arms of evil reached out from the shadowy old barn to draw us in.

We were both depressed and we were both tired. It had been a trying day, full of frustration. The walk up from the bay was hot, and I was short of sleep. The semidarkness of the big interior was grateful and the temperature a pleasant change. As our eyes grew accustomed to the shade, I marveled again at the fantastic catalogue of junk and jetsam that adorned the walls and ceiling. The compact usefulness of Mr. Snow's assortment offered no comparison, for in the barn-garage, the decorations were grotesque in their total irrelevance. Mr. Dali would have liked it.

There was the moose head, sneering down from semi-darkness, while the sweeps of some forgotten shell rose like long fingers to greet him. From the crossbeams hung the children's sleds, all of a bygone pattern; below the rooftree in the center was the weird shape of the pendent schoolroom chair. As I glanced at it, it seemed, despite the weight of foot and base, to sway a little in a secret breeze. A tiny chill ran down my back.

"The truck was parked right here, wasn't it?" Lucy was pointing to the empty space alongside the Corvette. For a moment she seemed to have forgotten her brother in the recollection of her own escape.

"There's quite a collection of footprints," I told her. "Tennis shoes, women's wear—"

"I see one I know!" She was pointing to the floor beside her in the center of the middle stall. "See!" she cried. "Those prints are—"

As she spoke, there came a rumbling sound from overhead and, on the instant, an appalling slam. The rope that held the schoolroom chair had parted, and the ironclad antique had plunged from upper darkness to the floor of the garage, its heavy plate less than six inches from where Lucy stood.

The building quivered and was still.

"Let's get out of here," Lucy said. Then in the sunlight, where the grass was green and only a cloud of golden motes told of the fallen monster, she reached out and grabbed my hand.

98

"Posy," she said, "I'm afraid I'm not a very safe girl for you to look after."

I didn't check on whether or not the rope had been cut, for I, too, knew to whom the puglike bootprints belonged. In the moment of near catastrophe, I had remembered seeing them —and on the living hoof.

Chapter

16

We went into the house after that, rather too weary and exhausted to plan anything. Mrs. Simpson was alone in the kitchen and gladly brewed us a pot of tea.

> *"Better by far for young and old*
> *Than potions poisonously cold."*

Such was her blessing on our refreshment.

"You stay here with Mrs. Simpson," I told Lucy. "I've got to make a phone call."

"I doubt if you will," said Mrs. S. "The line was out of order half an hour ago. I tried it myself, and if you ask me, it's this fancy up-Cape dial business has put the kibosh on what used to be a convenience. Seven numbers to remember—it's outrageous! And that there code business! Anybody'd think we were all spies!"

Since I had suffered in many places and for many years from the absurdities of telephonic advance, I could understand the resentment of the good lady whose down-Cape habitat had but lately been threatened by the newest edition of Bell's Madness.

"I'll come with you," said Lucy, and I took it to be an order. "Are you going to call the police, Posy?" In the hall she stopped me, eager to talk. "Don't you see it won't do any good? The trouble's *here!*" She looked about her, and her eye fell on the casket by the laboratory door. This time the *kilim* lay in a heap beside it. But what fascinated me seemed to be to her merely one among many discrepancies, a thing out of place among all things out of place. "It's here, right around us. Can't you feel it, Posy? It's nothing the police know about. It's something going on right in this house."

I thought of the staid Mrs. Simpson and her telephone troubles. But in grim contrast to her coziness, I saw in mind the dust rising in an angry cloud from the smitten floor of the garage, and the picture of Jamshid came to me, crouched like a priest over his flaming brazier.

"How long has it been going on?" I asked.

"Oh, for a long time, Posy. I don't know how long. Warburton noticed it first, a month or two after Daddy died. I can remember exactly what he said—you know how Warburton likes words: 'We are entering,' he said, 'a phase of malignancy.' And he explained what he meant, and I understood him perfectly."

"What *did* he mean?"

"He meant being scared when you went to bed—not of the old things like shadows and noises but of people and plans and what would be there in the morning. He meant wondering all the time—not natural wonders, like when the world will end or why they drown spare kittens, but bad things about good people and whether you could trust them any more. He meant looking at the sky for thunder instead of for birds."

She hesitated, then went on. "And then there were the Happenings—'our eldritch days' Warburton called them— like the time Mrs. Simpson found some white stuff in the sugar bowl that wasn't sugar, and like the day Cutty forgot and nearly shut me in my statue, and, oh, Posy, you've noticed —you must have noticed—just since you came: the truck, the clamps on *Bluejacket,* that awful, awful chair . . . and now Warburton's gone."

She didn't cry, but she was as close to it as I had ever seen her.

"I am going," I said, "to call the police."

I spoke firmly and rather loudly, for the mood of caution had left me; my hesitancy was gone; somebody simply *had* to do something.

The study phone was nearest. We had closed the door of that room when we went to the beach. In consequence, it never occurred to me to knock. I grasped the knob, pushed the door open, and walked in. For a moment the room seemed dark; then total darkness flooded around me as a black enveloping hood descended over my head and face. At the same moment, my arms were pinioned to my sides by an encircling band like steel. From somewhere behind me, I heard a squeal of terror—after that, silence.

I tried my best to cry out, but my voice was wholly muffled by the thing over my head. The more I strained to free my arms, the tighter grew the strap that bound them. I started to turn around—at least my feet were free—but strong hands grasped my shoulders; a kick from behind shot my legs out from under me; and with sure, swift purpose, my ankles were bound together.

Trussed like a pigeon for the stuffing, I was picked up bodily from the floor. I tried thrashing sideways, but it made no difference: they simply swung me like a hammock. When I felt that they were moving, I drew up my knees, pulling the foot-end carrier briefly closer. Then I let fly with both feet, hoping to ram him backward. But it didn't work; he gave with my kick and so alertly that I barely touched his body.

Abruptly, a surface of some sort was slipped underneath me, and while one pair of hands held me down, another strapped me to it. When it came to straps, these boys were well provided. And I had become a stretcher case.

Again I was lifted and began to move head-first—as I supposed—along the hall. Now we turned and now we turned again, but swathed and hog-tied as I was, I had lost all sense of direction. If my conductors engaged in any comment, I could not hear it. Nor did the sound of feet or furniture come through the stuffy folds of my nose bag.

The stretcher slanted, my weight shifting downward in the straps. Progress became more jerky, and I realized that I was being carried up a flight of stairs. I knew of two in the house: one mounted from the downstairs hall by several turns to the principal bedrooms; the other was the ascent to the children's bedrooms and my own abode. We kept straight upward, leveled off again, and journeyed on. It was pretty early, I thought, to be put to bed.

But for bed I was destined. As by some sort of signal, the supporting hands at either end of me gave way. Stretcher and all, I was dropped—to land full length on a flat but springy surface where I bounced a small bounce and then lay still.

It is an odd fact that I was not particularly frightened. I have noticed many times that action directed against myself—while it may be unexpected and unpleasant—rouses in me a reaction very different from what I feel when somebody else is in trouble. In the latter circumstance, I am jumpy, anxious, and ineffective—and these in some degree had been my states of mind since coming to Sexton's Prim. Now that the Amalekites were after *me*, I felt a kind of relief: I was angry and, in a strange way, entertained.

Lying on the bedded stretcher, I remembered a conversation long before at home. An older friend of my father's, a certain Mr. Audubon, had been held up one night after a quiet bridge game. With him at the time were two others from the foursome, an elderly brother and sister of unimpeachable propriety. The worthy trio had approached Mr. Audubon's car for the journey home and found it occupied by the thug—who made them enter, took their money, and deposited them on a distant street corner. As a small boy, I had heard the story, and encountering its victim not long after, I had asked him whether he hadn't been terribly scared. I can still hear his answer. "It was not," he said, "the terror. It was the indignity."

Something of Mr. Audubon's indignity—and of his indignation—had transferred itself to me during my journey under wraps.

I felt fingers fumbling at my throat—in an effort, I am glad to say, to loosen my headstall. Breathing was suddenly a good deal easier, and I thought that I could hear sounds of movement in the room.

I lay perfectly still. It might be fun to let them think I was unconscious.

A voice—disguised as well as muffled by my coverings—called me by name. "Flower," it said. "Flower! Listen to what I have to tell you."

I said nothing and showed no reaction.

"Flower! Can you hear me? If you can hear me, move the fingers on your left hand."

I kept my fingers perfectly still. (They were almost numb in any case from the tightness of the unrelenting straps.)

My unresponsive state, I told myself, might possibly move my captors to concern.

Not a bit of it. One of them stuck me in the buttock with what must have been a hatpin.

A restricted but emphatic jump on my part betrayed no lack of consciousness.

"Don't try any games on me," said the voice. (I noticed the "me"—not "us.") Then the mood of the speaker altered. Unless I was very much mistaken, the words were edged with laughter.

"It gives me pain to inconvenience you. It will be only for a time—until, in fact, you are discovered. But, for a time, you **are unnecessary**—you are not needed, Mr. Flower. In certain respects you are an inconvenience. And it is simply that you are less inconvenient here in your own bed. One would not wish you to miss the coming evening's diversions. But a measure of restraint seems indicated."

What a gabby guy, I thought—though the tone was so garbled that I could not be sure whether the speaker was a man or a woman. But if I could hear, I could presumably be heard.

"Afraid I won't like your looks?" I asked. My mouth was half filled with a coarse stuff like canvas. "Or are you a Faceless Fury," I persisted, "right out of the comic books?"

My visitor was not amused.

"Very funny," said the voice. "Very funny indeed. Perhaps it will enhance your good humor to know that only a special circumstance keeps you alive. I have already said you are an inconvenience. At any time, it may become advisable to change your—er—category."

"Nicely put," I commented.

"I may also tell you," the voice continued, "that your bonds are so arranged as to tighten as you struggle. This is particularly true of the fastenings at your throat. The less you move, the less difficulty you will have in breathing. Is it not good of me to let you know?"

"Most kind," I said, wishing that I could punch the face behind the oily chatter.

"Now," the voice told me, "I shall leave you for a time."

"Make it a time and a half," I answered.

There was no response.

I squirmed in my double harness and emitted several rudenesses. It was evident that my captors had taken themselves off. I tried relaxing and relaxed as well as I was able. The temporary spurt of courage had subsided, and I jumped at the sound of a heavy truck roaring, apparently, into the drive. The sound of its snorting mingled with a series of dull, thumping noises. Once, as from a great distance, I thought I heard a man shouting. Someone came and went below, whistling for his supper. I began to wonder what had happened to Lucy.

Sadly and stiffly, I fell asleep.

Chapter

17

It was a headache, I think, that woke me up. Or perhaps it was the sound of someone in the room.

I was not actually aware, however, that I had a visitor until I felt someone fumbling with the thing around my neck. There was a push against my forearm—and it was free! The bands that bound me to the stretcher were unloosed, and the strap that held my wrists to my side had been removed. The circulation in my hands began, rather painfully, to resume its normal course. Operations began on my ankles, and after a moment, I was able to part them, though stiffly. Again the hands went to my head. There were several objectionable tugs and twists; then the hood was pulled up and away, and my half-blind eyes blinked out at the half-dark room.

I must have been asleep some hours, for the afternoon had quite vanished, and the window—from which I noticed that the screen had been removed—hung against the wall like a pale picture. Against the twilit rectangle, there stood the silhouetted figure of a man, close beside my bed. Of medium height and active build, he wore a crush hat low on his forehead. His profile was completed by a short and cocky beard. As far as I could tell, I had never seen him before in my life.

"May I inquire," I said, "as to the purpose of your attentions?"

My visitor moved away from the window, and I could see him a little better. His dark, rather shaggy suit consisted of jacket and plus fours. Without doubt, this was Lucy's Gnome. For a moment I thought that his eyes gleamed; then I realized that he was wearing dark glasses.

"I am deeply indebted," I told him, "for your courtesy in rousing me. I do not usually sleep in such complicated bed-clothes."

He chuckled, and there was something oddly familiar about the chuckle. Then he spoke, and the instant he spoke, I *knew*. The hat, the clothes, even the face were those of a stranger, but the voice I could not mistake.

I had never before seen my father with a beard.

"I'm glad to observe that your spirits are undaunted," he said. "I'd have been here sooner, but I wanted to see Lucy. She seems, for the moment, to be mislaid. Quite a girl you've got there."

I was running over with questions. Relief at his appearance vied with avid curiosity.

"I got your wire," I said, "but I didn't know when to expect you."

"And you observed the 'hush'? You didn't tell anyone about hearing from me?"

I shook my head.

"Good. You seem to have acted wisely from the first."

"But all sorts of awful things are happening," I told him.

"I know. I probably know more about the awful things than you do. This is a grand house to find things out in. When they put you so neatly to bed, for instance, I was listening to them on the squawk box in the doctor's study. And by the way, you shouldn't have left that crumpled letter on the doctor's desk after you and Lucy had read it. I put it back in the wastebasket—after I unbugged the bugging job."

"But how—how did you know—?"

"I know you've a hundred questions to ask, and there's nothing I'd rather do than sit here for a friendly chat. Unfortunately, there is—in Mr. G. M. Cohan's immortal words—'work to be done, to be done,' and I'm afraid I'll have to assign some of it to you. You'll get an answer to the questions soon enough.

"Now hear this. There is a vehicle—with driver—waiting for you behind the studio. I want you to go where you are taken and ask no questions. However, to the first person who says to you, 'Gambit,' you are to reply, 'Excalibur.' Got that?"

"Indeed, yes. 'Gambit' and 'Excalibur.' Am I likely to meet someone who says 'Gambit'? I'm sorry. What then?"

"If the question is asked, 'Alone or together?'—you are to reply, 'Alone.' You will be told *what*, then."

"But," I protested, the questions bursting out after all, "what about Warburton? Do you know about him? He's been kidnapped or something, and I never reached the police, and Mrs. Budding doesn't even know—"

"These are matters that must wait." When he speaks in that tone, his mouth shuts like a trap, and I know better than to spring it.

"Then just this," I begged. "Where is everybody—I mean Dr. Sarx and Mrs. Budding and all?"

"Dr. Sarx and Mrs. Budding are finishing their dinner, waited upon by the remarkable Jamshid. There is a rumor about that you have taken the children off on a picnic. The chauffeur—whatever his name is—has gone to the village. He seems to go to the village a good deal. But then I suppose he and the two Egyptians are exhausted by this afternoon's activities."

"What activities?"

He laughed shortly. "During your rest period, old boy, we celebrated moving day at Sexton's Prim. Uncle Cutty has transferred a number of his deathless works from the studio to the laboratory. Means? The Egyptians. Plus moving men from Chatham—latter mystified. Plus me—thought by village varlets to be part of staff—thought by staff to be village varlet. Motive? Who can tell?"

He made a clicking sound of self-reproach. "My erstwhile downy couch and dwelling place has also departed," he told me. "Charlie the Charioteer—*that's* his name!—took it to Hyannis. On my orders, I'm afraid."

"Your downy couch?" I didn't understand.

"We're wasting time," he said. "I shall be off downstairs, hoping to encounter no one—unless it's Lucy. You will take my entrance route."

He gestured to the window, which was now a square of darkness. Still stiff in legs and arms, I walked over to it and looked out. A pruning ladder leaned against the sill and led downward into the night.

"Get going," said my father, and I clambered out of the opening. In and out the window, I thought to myself, all the day long. Once overside, I ventured a final question.

"How did you get here anyway—into the house, I mean?"

His laugh this time was alarmingly loud.

"You carried me in yourself, Jonathan. Last night. In the casket. Really very comfortable what with an oxygen portable and Sarx's supersilk upholstery."

Chapter

18

I did not bother to remove the ladder. My father had not mentioned it, and I felt sure that he would have if it really mattered. Besides, I was filled now with a sense of urgency—a consciousness of necessary action—which was not to leave me for the rest of that memorable night.

A pale moon was rising over the invisible Atlantic, and behind me lights shone out from the kitchen and rear quarters. The laboratory windows were quite dark.

"Behind the studio," my father had said: there I would find my chariot. I skirted the breezeway and headed for the corner of the big black outbuilding. There was my chariot, right enough, glistening dimly in the moonlight. It was, of all things, an electric brougham—make, Daimler; vintage, 1904—boxy and beautiful. Then and there the night took on an aura of magnificent absurdity. The car—a gallant little vehicle out of the olden time—was something from dreamland; and so was the arm, clad in white samite (or something very like it) that reached out to open a door and beckon me inside.

" 'The splendor falls on castle walls,' "

said a voice with which I was becoming reasonably familiar.

" *'Life, like a dome of many-colored glass,'* "

quoted Mrs. Little, mixing up her poets—

" *'Stains the white radiance of Eternity.'* "

The little electric was not precisely a dome of many-colored glass, but the similarity made it a near thing. Exquisitely soft upholstery prompted me to think of my father's recent journey. Mrs. Little pressed a switch, and with no noise at all the quaint contraption began to move. Over hummocks and hillocks we bumped and bounced, my elderly conductress having in mind no man-made route; cheerily, she steered with one hand on the tiller (for there was no wheel); and as she steered, she sang, her music skipping a couple of generations:

" *'There's a long, long trail a-winding . . .'* "

Her voice, as I had had occasion to note earlier, was high and reedy. But I must admit that it perfectly suited the moon and the landscape. And to her own strange accompaniment, Mrs. Little drove her brougham like a tank. There were no lights on the car, but their lack made no matter. Onward we went at a steady, silent pace, up hill and down dale, swiping serenely at bushes, jouncing over stones, losing traction for a moment in a sand patch, nearly being turned over by an outthrust root—onward under the moon until the house was out of sight and we had somehow circled it to head northwest over the banks and braes.

" *'Somewhere, somewhere,*
Beautiful isle of somewhere . . .' "

Mrs. Little sang, and the moonlight gave me intermittent glimpses of her face. For half the time, as far as I could see, her eyes were closed, but her expression, as usual, was both buoyant and enthusiastic. It never occurred to me to wonder whether she had a destination.

But suddenly, we stopped.

"Here we are, here we are," said Mrs. Little. *"Hier stehe ich, ich kann nichts anderes.* Don't you agree that Luther was a great man?"

"Indeed I do," I assured her.

"A poet *manqué,* perhaps?" Moonlight fell beside her window on a small glass vase. It was filled with nasturtiums.

"Well," I said. "He did pretty well with *Ein' feste Burg.*"

She pounced on the chorale and made it her own, singing this time in a low tenor, which I had not heard before.

A realization of our errand seemed to strike her. With one slim hand, she pushed back white and wispy hair. With the other, she pointed toward an opening in the nearby poplar thicket.

I dismounted—no other word seems appropriate—and the little car took off soundlessly into the night.

We had stopped by a sizable grove of clustering poplars. The moonlight silvered the underside of their leaves, and the opening toward which Mrs. Little had pointed was an uninviting black hole. I gathered, however, that this was to be my route, and bending low to avoid the branches, I entered the darkness.

The trail was a veritable tunnel, lightened only here and there by a filter of moonshine. For someone Lucy's size, treading it in broad daylight, it might have been an easy road to follow. For me, it was both difficult and disagreeable. Whippy branches cut across my face, and I stumbled repeatedly over roots and undergrowth. Only the fact that the path was straight kept me from losing it entirely.

I had gone, I suppose, some fifty yards when far ahead of me, at what I hoped was the end of the tunnel, I saw a light. Not a very bright one, to be sure, but a sign of life.

With a target to aim at, I made a little better time. Puffing and panting, I gained the end of the underpass. But the light, which I now made out to be a lantern, had moved on ahead of me and beckoned me to follow. As if this were not sufficiently frustrating, the silly fool of a will-o'-the-wisp began to run.

Happily, it was the last lap. The lantern came to a stop, and so, with a few more breathless strides, did I. My guide and I were standing in the shadow of a big, dark house. I guessed that it was Gannet Lodge. Profoundly curious, I peered over the lantern at the face of its bearer. Even then I couldn't believe my eyes. It was Mrs. Little again, my erstwhile *chauffeuse*, grinning and blinking at me like a woolly lemur.

"Good lad," she cackled, very *sotto voce*. "Well done. Well done. 'Though the way be rough and dreary.' And so on. I drove around to meet you, you see. We couldn't have you coming through the front of the house with Cordelia's little friends all there, could we now?"

Cordelia? Then I remembered that Cordelia was Chicken's real name. Apparently, I had missed a party.

"No," I said. "We certainly couldn't."

"This way," said the lady with the lamp. She shaded the lantern—it was an old-fashioned bull's-eye—and set it on the ground. Then she began prying at a slanted cellar door. I bent to help her, and we opened the upper leaf.

"The steps," she said, "are very dark."

They certainly were.

"No more tunnels?" I asked. It was half hope, half question.

"There's a light switch," she told me. "Right across the room. But don't use it, dear boy, till I've shut the door again. Ha-ha-ha! 'Oft in danger, oft in woe!' Ha-ha-ha!" She raised the lantern again, and it cast a glimmer of light on my take-off into the abyss.

I felt my way down the steps and heard the cellar door slam behind me. In the absolute black, I bumped into a box or bench and gave my shin a crack I can still feel. A wall came up and met my outstretched hands. I groped along it, and sure enough, my fingers encountered an extruded switch plate. I used it, and a dim and dirty bulb—all of twenty-five watts was my guess—sprang to life and revealed a rather grubby, but perfectly normal, cellar room.

The walls were of undressed stone, the low ceiling propped here and there on ancient tree trunks from which the bark had long ago departed. The floor was clear—except for the bench with which I had collided so unerringly—but an atmosphere of dampness and decay pervaded the whole chamber. At one end an archway led into a passage, which I followed past a boiler pit and a great cast-iron furnace. At the far end of this engineroom, a door, its paint comparatively new, suggested entrance into living quarters. I pushed it open and found myself in the bright light of one of those basement *bierstuben* repulsively known as "rumpus rooms." The floor was linoleum tile; a bar slanted across one corner; a pair of lengthy couches lined the walls. Needless to say, there was a television set.

And seated at a table in the center of all this was Mr. Francis Torquil, playing himself a game of chess. He must have heard my entrance, but he did not look around.

"Hello," he said. "K to K's 4. No, that won't do. Do you play chess?"

"A bit," I admitted. "Nothing fancy, though."

"Maybe you can help me," he said. "Opponent opened with Ostrakoff's gambit."

"Try the 'Excalibur' defense," I suggested.

"Alone or together?" he inquired—with decidedly small relevance, it seemed to me.

"Alone," I told him. He pushed the table away and turned to me with a smile of relief.

"There," he said. "Good. We've said our piece. Though why the Major had to lay such ghastly, complicated plans, I'll never understand."

"Perhaps he didn't know that we had met."

"Perhaps not. That's a good backhand you have. Anyway, I always do exactly what he says."

"So do I," I said, "usually." I had had no idea that he was one of my father's many curious friends. "You don't work for him, do you? I mean—you're not in the same office or something?"

Mr. Torquil smiled again. "Not exactly. Let's say we've had professional contacts. How did you get along with Aunt Megan?"

"Aunt Megan? Oh, is Mrs. Little your aunt?" He seemed altogether too conventional for so spectacular a relative. "We —er—managed," I said.

"Wonderful girl," he assured me. "Wonderful girl and wonderful car." He looked at his wrist watch. "It's getting on. And I dare say you know we're due at the Sexton's Prim gate a little before eleven."

"*We*'re due! But I thought— Isn't that when and where they want the money—the people who've taken Warburton?"

"I believe so." His manner was suddenly languid.

My protest, I'm afraid, showed irritation. "I just wish somebody would let me in on this business. Why in heaven's name don't we send for the police? What's the sense of letting Dr. Sarx play sucker—and find out he's wrong when it's too late? I'll go along on almost anybody's moonlit ride; but I've already been on one—I've been on one for three days, it seems to me—and I think I'm entitled to an explanation!"

"You're probably hungry," said Mr. Torquil.

He was quite right. I was. And my temper improved a little as from a small refrigerator behind the bar he produced three ham sandwiches and a bottle of milk.

"Here," he said, pouring me a glassful. "This'll make you feel better. But I'm afraid I can't answer your questions very well. All I know is what your father chose to tell me. Till this morning I hadn't seen him for months, and this morning I saw him only for minutes. He made some arrangements with me about this house, sent his love to Aunt Megan—whom he seems to know better than I do—and told me that 'things were coming to a head.' What things, I don't really know, except that he seems to hold your host in very low esteem."

"Why Dr. Sarx?" I asked, my mouth half full of sandwich. I didn't care much for the doctor, but he had been off and away whenever anything happened.

"I don't know why Dr. Sarx, but I gather that your father thinks he's some kind of madman. Anyway, you and I are supposed to be at the gate at eleven o'clock, where, I presume, we'll have the opportunity of observing the doctor in action. Your father said he would send me word tonight. Aunt Megan said she was going to 'fetch our visitor.' If the messenger passed the Excalibur test, I was to ask him, 'Alone or together?' And if he answered, 'Alone,' I was to take him along to the gate. Typical Flower perversity, if you ask me. I don't believe even the State Department can be sure when your father has—or has not—his tongue in his cheek."

I was busy filling in some gaps for myself. I had a pretty shrewd idea of when my father had made his arrangements with Aunt Megan. After all, Lucy had seen her Gnome down by the shore that very morning. I had some theories, too, about some other elements of mystery. But questions still came quicker than answers, and one big puzzle seemed as difficult as ever: if the source of evil lay at Sexton's Prim, who had snatched young Warburton? As for my father's eccentric role in the proceedings, I knew him well enough to be sure that he had his own reasons. Even the apparent foolishness of "Gambit" gave me a warranty of trust in someone whom I scarcely knew. Eccentric or not, I approved of my father the way he was.

"There is one matter"—Mr. Torquil spoke with a hint of apology in his tone—"there is one matter on which I think I can relieve your mind." He turned and, as it seemed, addressed the television set. "You can come out now, captain."

The mahogany cabinet quivered, and out from behind it—
quite as large as life and with no signs of damage in handling
—stepped Master Warburton Budding.

Chapter

19

"Good evening," he said. "I am not ordinarily an eavesdropper."

Relief and astonishment—in mixed quantities—held me speechless.

"I'm sorry, Posy, if I caused you much concern. What I did seemed for the best."

"Where have you been?" I asked him.

"Here for most of the time. I managed to work out two new gambits, didn't I, Mr. Torquil?"

Mr. Torquil nodded.

"But the kidnappers," I insisted. "What about them? Do you realize that your uncle at this moment is probably insane with anxiety. That by now the police (I hope) have been called—"

But I didn't really hope so any longer. The whole situation had turned upside down. I was almost relieved when Mr. Torquil interrupted, like a teacher in the schoolroom:

"Time enough for explanations later. Come along, gentlemen. It's half-past ten."

"Is this—is *he* going with us?" I wanted to know, pointing at my so-called charge.

"Indeed, yes," said Mr. Torquil. "I rather think the evening has just begun for Warburton. We'll use a side door. The house should be quiet by now. Follow me."

As a matter of fact, the house was not quiet. Someone was playing the piano, and as we climbed a flight of stairs to the kitchen, we heard voices raised in chorus. From the front of the house, there came a roar of laughter, then silence, then more laughter and a round of applause. Obviously, Chicken's party was in progress. There had, after all, been some reason in Mrs. Little's roundabout routing.

Silence again from the front of the house; then Chicken's alto all alone. Chicken Tetrazzini, I told myself. Her voice was better, but her repertoire was like her grandmother's. " 'Where is my wandering boy tonight?' " she sang, and I wondered how much she knew of the evening's involutions.

Mr. Torquil answered my thought in a whisper. "She made the sandwiches," he said. One up for Chicken. (Only they were ham.)

The door by which we let ourselves out gave on a driveway, and I reckoned that we were now on the side of the house nearest the tennis court. Mrs. Little was nowhere to be seen, but her brougham awaited us, glossily rectangular under the moon.

Mr. Torquil made a sound of vague distaste. "Posy, can you run this machine?"

"I guess so," I said. It hadn't looked very complicated under Aunt Megan's hands.

"*I* can," said Warburton, showing neither hesitation nor reluctance. "I can, and I know the terrain. You guys'll break an axle. I'd better drive."

"How are we all going to get into it?" I asked. The car was distinctly a two-seater, and neither Mr. Torquil nor myself was small.

"We'll manage." Warburton was already in place, hands firmly on the steering bar, feet feeling for the brake. "This thing fits me very well."

Torquil and I jammed ourselves in beside him, and my second joy ride of the evening began. For a few hundred yards, Warburton—who, I must say, seemed to know what he was doing—kept us firmly on the drive, and with the moon full up, it was easy to see where we were going.

Abruptly, he turned onto rough ground, and the brougham broke into a kind of canter, reeling and bucking through the half-seen countryside at a hell-for-leather fifteen miles per hour. Conversation was impossible. Each of us hung on to any fixture he could find. And so we drove for ten enormous minutes.

"This should just about do us." Warburton had stopped the car on a level space bordered by sizable pines. "The gate's through there"—he pointed left, directly at the trees—"and there's our driveway coming down from Sexton's Prim." I followed his indication and could see a portion of road winding downhill in our direction.

My sense of geography reasserted itself. Both of my most recent auto trips had drawn a shortcut from house to house, or rather—in the case of trip number two—from Littles' house to Sarx's gate. Beyond the trees lay the main road from the village. Somewhere to our left ran the low wall that outlined Sexton's Prim.

"Let's go," said Torquil. "The car can't be seen from here, and the pines will make good cover."

So they did, and no sooner had we entered them, our feet quite silent on the mat of last year's needles, than—of all sounds to hear outdoors near midnight!—a phone began to ring. It was a dull and rusty ring, but the burr of it was unmistakable.

I had managed to move pretty well through the pines—practiced perhaps by my earlier forest scramble—and though but a single thickness of trees remained in front of me, I was well concealed. At the same time, I had a perfect view of wall and driveway and of the gate by which the latter gained the road. Behind me, I heard the others moving up.

"Don't budge a muscle till I tell you to." Mr. Torquil's whisper was fierce as a shout.

The phone rang again, and as I looked, a figure rose from behind the wall, vaulted lightly over, and stooped to where I guessed there was a stone receptacle.

"Hello?" His quiet voice was clearly audible on the night air. Then in the same low tone, he burst into a flood of Oriental language—Iranian, I thought—but much too fast for me to follow. The speaker was Lucy's Gnome, crush hat, short beard, and all.

I heard the phone click, and the man crossed the wall again and disappeared. Almost at once the headlights of a car threw up their radiance from the direction of the doctor's house. A bend in the driveway hid them; after a moment they appeared again, rapidly drawing nearer.

Some fifty yards short of the gate, the car stopped, and its lights went out. The crunch of footsteps sounded on the drive, closer and closer—and the portly figure of the doctor stood directly opposite our hiding place. No *jallabiyah* wrapped him round. The moon shone down on a white shirt front; for this night of derring-do, the doctor wore his dinner clothes.

He coughed. It was an artificial, telegraphic cough. "Here I am," it said. "Here I am, and where are you?"

The man outside the wall rose to sight. In his hand there was a gleam of metal. (I was surprised, for my father seldom carries a gun.) But it was my father's voice.

"Sarx?"

"Where's the boy?"

"There's a bet on that answer. Did you bring your stake?"

"I did, you villain. If you'd hit on any other night—"

"You wouldn't have bothered? Names won't help. Come

toward me six paces. One. Two. Three. Four. Five. Six. Drop the money there. Now back to where you were."

Torquil was whispering in my ear. "I'm off to fix his wagon," he said—and I understood that he meant it literally. "I may be back, but don't wait for me. After this is over, get up to the house as fast as you can. Take the brougham around back. 'Luck." I sensed his silent departure through the trees.

"What are you waiting for?" the Gnome asked Dr. Sarx.

"For the boy, of course."

"The boy will be delivered in due time. Go up to the house and wait there."

The doctor was furious. You could see it in the tenseness of his pose; you could hear it in his voice. "You have cheated me. You do not have the boy." A pause. "No one cheats Caspar Sarx."

With snakelike speed his hand moved to the back of his collar—then shot forward. A tracer trail of shining metal arrowed toward my father, and I doubt that anyone but me knew for the moment what had happened, for the knife disappeared against the darkness and there was neither sign nor sound of it until my father held it up, the blade shining in the moonlight. He had read Sarx's movement, bobbed the necessary inch, and caught the knife in flight by its handle.

"You telegraph your throw," he observed. "A pretty poor show for someone with your opportunities. Now be off with you." And to encourage his opponent, he fired a single shot in the direction of the doctor's feet.

Sarx broke and ran. But instead of heading back along the driveway toward his car, he turned and charged straight at the thicket of pines where Warburton and I kept watch. My father swung with the target but held his fire, realizing that we were in the spinney.

Dr. Sarx landed in between us. I'm sorry to say that something tripped him (probably Warburton), and he came down heavily. I say probably Warburton because that young man proceeded to sit on the doctor's neck and belabor his head with a pine faggot. The younger contestant showed every appearance of animus.

"What on earth goes on?" Mr. Torquil had returned. "Stop that, Warburton." He spoke in a quiet voice but with authority. "Dr. Sarx has an appointment at the house tonight. Ours not to say him nay."

He pulled Warburton off the prostrate doctor and felt the latter's head. "Out for a bit," was the cheerful diagnosis. "We'd better help him home. Posy, see if the coast's clear. Then bring the Cadillac as near as you can. Here are the keys. I borrowed them as a delaying action, but I didn't suppose you'd knock the brute out. There's no point in keeping them now. I simply wanted to make sure that Posy and I got back to the house ahead of the doctor. His present condition will give us plenty of time."

The doctor's dive had carried us all a few feet into the thicket. On order, I resumed my former observation post. There was no sign of my father, and I remarked that the white envelope Dr. Sarx had dropped had disappeared.

"All serene," I told the others. I felt sure that Mr. T. had recognized the Gnome. At any rate, he offered no suggestion of pursuit. I made for the Cadillac and let it drift downhill to our rendezvous. The three of us picked up Dr. Sarx and with some difficulty placed him back of his own wheel. The rotund figure slumped, and Mr. Torquil rearranged him.

"Really, Warburton," he said. "You made yourself some extra work." He fussed a minute with the doctor's tie till it sat square above the soiled dress shirt. (Each passing minute made me see more clearly why this man should be a friend of my father's.) "There. That should do. Yessir, you made yourself some extra work. *You* have to wake him up, you know." A moan escaped from the unconscious doctor, and Mr. Torquil drew us away from the car.

"If Sarx had behaved like a gentleman," he said, "the mysterious stranger would of course not have had to shoot. The idea was—"

"I know," Warburton interrupted. "The idea was that I'd be produced from the bushes—as per agreement."

"And the agreement will be kept. We leave you with the body and the body with you. When he comes to—any minute now, I'd guess—you can tell him you were dropped off at the gate—from a truck, I think—unless you feel a hearse would be more appropriate? Just remember to be glad to see him, deeply concerned at his wounding, and vague on your own captivity—quite the normal little nephew, catch?"

"I'm afraid," said Warburton, "I'll never be a normal little nephew."

I agreed but said nothing. I was anxious to be off before our victim waked and spotted us. But the boy wasn't satisfied. "Who, by the way"—he wanted to know—"*is* the Mysterious Stranger?"

"It's Captain Nemo," said Mr. Torquil. "He just swam over from Hyannisport. See you later."

The jester and I walked back around the spinney to the brougham. I must confess that I felt rather sorry for Warburton. No doubt he knew more than I did of the plan by which we were performing. On the other hand, Dr. Sarx was hardly likely to be at his best on waking, and from what I had seen of him, he was not my ideal of a baby-sitter. But who was I to talk?

"You ought to be able to drive this thing," said Mr. Torquil. "Turn the switch, and nature does the rest."

I pulled open the door of the brougham.

"Come right in," said my father from the dim interior.

Chapter

20

I remember once reading in a British list of precedence ("Who comes first—a duke or a marquis?"—that sort of thing) that mere "Companions" of various orders give place in a parade to "Masters in Lunacy." An interesting, and very British, ruling. I mulled it over on our way to the doctor's house. It seemed to me that my mastership was well nigh won, for surely a madder night has seldom been than the one in which I was involved. I could not see—I could not even guess at the real sense of it. My father and Mr. Torquil seemed to know what they were doing, but they also seemed possessed of a vast number of facts that I had not.

We skirted the house and disembarked behind the studio—where I had first beheld the brougham. Lights shone from the kitchen quarters, and we could see a glow stretching away from the windows of the living room.

"Do you suppose," I asked my father, "that Mrs. Budding knows where the doctor went—and why?"

"I think I told you," he said, "that *you* were supposed to be out with both the children. I dare say she thinks it's high time you were back."

"Oh, come now," Mr. Torquil protested, "Elizabeth wouldn't—"

"Elizabeth wouldn't mind a visit from you, lover-boy. Late as it is, you can say that you've just driven over to see whether everything's all right. There was a rumor in the village, don't you remember, that someone had called the police from Sexton's Prim. You won't have seen Sarx, of course; in fact, you'll be surprised to hear he's out; and you'll not know anything about the children. During your cozy chat, Warburton ought to arrive with his casualty. From there in, you'll just play it by ear. I'm hoping the good doctor will invite you to the Unveiling."

"You think he'll go ahead with it?" Torquil's question was Greek to me.

"I do indeed. The little matter of a knock on the head won't deter him—particularly when the decans are fulfilled."

"Decans? What on earth are they?" I asked.

"They're star readings, positions of the constellations, visible for ten days at a time. The Egyptians set great store by them. Of course, he might proceed in a different spirit if he knew who'd given him the knock. That Warburton!" My father came close to clucking. "But we have jobs to do. You may as well get around and pay your call at once, Torquil. We'll be along to eavesdrop after a bit.

"Posy, I want you take care of the cars. Leave the brougham alone, but immobilize the rest. Who'd have the spare keys?"

"Charlie Vickers," I said.

"A good egg," said my father.

"One of the best."

"Then get the extra keys from him and tell him to keep an eye on the brougham. No one's to take it unless I say so. Is that clear?"

"Yessir." It is always the proper answer when he turns into a field marshal. "What then?"

"Then meet me right back here. I've got to see to Jamshid."

I wasn't sure what he meant, but I knew what I'd like him

to mean. "Give him a couple for me," I said, and I hurried away toward the dark bulk of the garage.

Halfway there, I decided to see if Charlie was at home. I knew that his was one in the row of servants' rooms that gave inside the house onto the corridor I have described as leading to my stairway. Two of them also had doors directly onto the lawn where I stood, and one of these doorways was lighted. I gave it a try, and sure enough, Charlie answered.

"Oh," he said. "Hee-hee. It's you." His tone was one of relief. "Did you get back with the kids all right? You didn't take no car."

For the first time in far too long, I thought of Lucy. Surely my father must have found her, stowed her somewhere safely? But he hadn't said anything about it. I hoped for the best. This was no time for long explanations.

"As far as I know, the kids are fine," I said. "But I'm supposed to check on the cars. Do you have all the keys?"

"Doctor's got the Cadillac," he said.

"So he does. That accounts for one set. How about the other cars and the spare keys to the Caddy?"

"I've got 'em," he said. "Includin' the Corvette, where you left a set in the dash. I thought maybe you was goin' to use them. Then I figured I'd better pick 'em up."

"Good. And the spares?"

"There's a set for the Corvette and the Caddy and the truck —there always is—sittin' in my dresser drawer." He gestured behind him. "Right where I can always find 'em." (And right where any other person in the know can help himself, I thought.)

"What's up?" he asked.

"Plenty, apparently. All kinds of things have happened, and—I'm supposed to be hurrying, Charlie. Come along with me to the garage, and I'll tell you what I know."

He nodded. We had been talking through his screen door. Now he opened it and joined me in the moonlight.

"It's that feller calls himself John Dillinger," he said, "the spry little man in short pants. Hee-hee. Seems to have kind of taken charge around here. Funny thing, last Dillinger I heard of was a hold-up man or something. Anyway, this one gives orders like he means it. Sent me down to Hyannis with one of the boxes today. Shipping orders was O.K., though: they expected me. Know who he is?"

"I do, Charlie, and all I can say now is that we've got to trust him."

"Figured that for myself. Feels sorta good to have somebody to trust around here—what with all this foreign talk and heathen people, you might say. I ain't been too happy lately—been feelin' like the place was goin' to blow up! Know what I mean?"

We had reached the garage where the Moskvitch 430 stood beside the Corvette. There were keys in neither, and Charlie rattled the bunch in his pocket.

"I'm glad you have them all," I said. "My—er—Mr. Dillinger wants to be sure no one can take a car out tonight without his knowing. Will you hear the doctor when he gets back?"

"Will if I stick around here," said Charlie. "That's just what I'll do—stick around here. The doctor usually leaves his keys in—expects me to collect 'em about midnight. Past that now, I betcha. I'll collect 'em all right."

My watch corroborated him.

"Fine, Charlie." I was anxious to get back to my father. "But there's one other thing. When you have all the keys, you're to go back of the studio and stand guard over Mrs. Little's brougham. Understand?"

"Mrs. Little's—you mean the electric? What on earth's that doing here—that telephone booth on wheels?"

"It's a long story, but don't let anybody take it, will you?"

"Do my best," said Charlie. Which was all I wanted to know.

Leaving my watchman on guard, I rounded the corner of the garage and observed that the ladder was still in place beneath my window. No one, apparently, had noticed this handy fire escape, and for a moment I debated whether or not to leave it in place.

As I pondered, a very small voice hailed me from above.

"Posy! Is that you?" It was Lucy calling from my window.

I wasn't very anxious for a second-story conversation, so I told her to come down. "Crawl out the window and come down the ladder."

"I never even knew it was there," she told me, a little out of breath from her hurried descent. "I've been looking out the window for ever so long, and then I saw you in the moonlight. I was sure it was you."

"Well, you certainly wouldn't want to call from a bedroom window to perfect strangers. And by the way, what were you doing in *my* room?"

"The Gnome put me in there," she said.

I marveled at the omnipresence of my father.

"You see," she went on, "when you went into the study this afternoon to telephone, I waited behind you in the hall. I was going to follow you in, but I heard a queer noise—as if you had fallen or something—and just then somebody grabbed me from behind and clapped a bag over my head."

"I got the same treatment," I said. "But it couldn't have been the Gnome."

"Oh no! *He* was afterward. You see, they took me up to my own room and locked me in—still with the bag on. I could breathe all right, and I could recognize the furniture by feeling it. But I couldn't make much noise, and it really was awfully annoying. Besides, I was worried about you."

I was touched by her concern but also curious. "Did you see who grabbed you?" I asked.

"No, I didn't. And I must have been in my room for perfect

ages—until the Gnome came and switched me into yours. I think he's awfully nice."

I knew that it was important for me to get back to my father, but her story was most intriguing. "He switched you into my room?"

"Yes. He said nobody'd look for me there, and he was going to lock my room again from the outside, so they'd think I was perfectly safe. Who is he, Posy? He's simply *got* to be a good guy."

"He is," I said. "But look here, Lucy—I have to do something with you." (It might even be better, I thought, to send her back up the ladder.) "All kinds of things seem to be popping—"

"I want to pop, too," she said. "Don't just *put* me somewhere: I've been *put* for hours."

"I know," I told her. "You can help Charlie Vickers watch the cars." But when we had walked around the end of the barn, Charlie Vickers was nowhere in sight.

Almost at once, however, he appeared from the nearest clump of trees and greeted us.

"Didn't know who you was," he explained. "Lucy, what you doin' up?"

I told him how she and I had met and that we both would like him to keep her company for a while. He took this rather peculiar request like a lamb and asked no questions. Lucy was less amenable.

"One thing more, Posy. What about—is there any more news about Warburton?"

"I have reason to believe," I said, "that Warburton is all right. I can't tell you more now."

And so I left them, seeking cover where their view of the garage would be unimpeded but where they themselves would remain unseen. As I turned away, the sound of a car could be heard on the drive, and headlights glowed over the nearest hill. I hoped it was the doctor coming home. It was a little late for strange visitors.

21

My father was waiting just about where I had left him.

"What's been keeping you?" he wanted to know. "Sarx has arrived. He doesn't look very happy. I hope Warburton didn't hit him too hard."

"I don't think so. Wasn't he able to drive?"

"He arrived behind the wheel all right, but Warburton had to help him land. They left the Cadillac out front. What'd you do about the keys?"

I told him briefly of my arrangements with Charlie and of Lucy's reappearance.

"Good," he said. "I wanted to get her out of that room, but I haven't had time. Vickers will have sense enough to take care of the doctor's car?"

"I'm sure he will. He'll see it perfectly from where he's stationed."

"Good. Then the next thing is for you to keep a watch on the people in the living room. I shan't be about for a bit: I've some make-up work to do. But I've got to know when they make their move. It'll be your job to warn me—with this."

He pressed into my hand an object that felt like a slender egg.

"Just a minute," I said. (There are times when you absolutely *have* to slow my father down.) "Who's going to make what move?"

"*They* are—the doctor, Mrs. B., and Warburton. Torquil, too, if he's been asked to stay. Otherwise, he's to say good night and pretend to go home. In which case, he will actually join you. Oh, and of course the *fellahin* may be involved—I haven't seen them all evening."

"And where are they all going?"

"I'm coming to that. They're all going to the lab, where, if I'm not mistaken, the doctor plans to give a demonstration."

"Of what?"

"Of magic, in a way. You know—'The seal of the pack is unbroken. I will ask one gentleman to break the seal, another to cut the pack'—that sort of thing. The point is, you've got to be in the lab ahead of them. Listen as long as you think you're safe; learn all you can; signal me; then beat it—into the lab as quick as a minute and up into the balcony."

"Balcony?" But then, of course, my visit to the super-secret chamber had been at best by flashlight: I had no idea of the room's upper regions.

"Yes. Didn't you—? No. I suppose not. The balcony is right across from the door. There's a small spiral staircase in the corner farthest from you as you enter. Make for that and tuck yourself away up there, and don't do anything else till you hear from me. Right?"

"Right."

"Oh"—as an afterthought—"the lab'll be unlocked." He slid away into the darkness, and I moved around the corner of the house, keeping just far enough away to escape the patches of light thrown by the living-room windows. The sound of conversation—or, at the moment, monologue—came to me clearly. Dr. Sarx was speaking, apparently to Warburton:

"It is very good to have you back, my boy. You and your sister are essential to what I have in mind tonight. It's a good

thing Mother doesn't know all about our adventures—eh?"
He was making heavy work of joviality.

"I don't understand at all." It was Mrs. Budding speaking.
"I thought you were with Posy, Warburton—you and Lucy
both. Now you come back with Uncle Caspar, and you two
look as if you'd been in a war. And what have you done with
Lucy?"

Dr. Sarx made confident answer. "Lucy will be with us any
minute now." If this were sheer bluff, he was putting up a
remarkably good show.

"And what about Posy?" persisted Mrs. Budding. "He
didn't just go off to bed, did he?"

The doctor chuckled. "I shouldn't be surprised if that's
exactly what he's done. Ah, Jamshid, there you are. Where is
Lucy?"

There was a low murmur, which I took to be the butler's
voice. Then the doctor's, raised in protest: "Not there? Of
course she's there! You say the door to her room was locked—
on the outside?"

"Oh, dear," lamented Mrs. Budding. "I *knew* I ought to
have gone up—but you were so sure, Caspar, so absolutely
positive the children were with Posy! There's something
awfully queer about this. You *told* me she was out. Then why
did you send Jamshid to look in Lucy's room? And why
are you surprised she isn't there? I should think the logical
thing—"

"The logical thing—the logical thing—" Dr. Sarx laughed
rather nastily. "There, Mr. Torquil, speaks reasonable
womanhood." To Mrs. B.: "Of course, my dear. Without a
doubt you're right. Lucy and that Flower boy are on their way
home—I don't question it—sorry to be late, no doubt, but
safe in each other's company."

There was a stridency to his voice now; he spoke with the
driven note of one under great pressure. "Too bad—that they
are late, that is. It interferes with our completeness. I had

planned so perfect an occasion. Do me the favor, will you, Mr. Torquil, to step outside and read the moon? Right here, by the French windows. Sothis and the decans reappear tonight. Just let me know the elevation, will you? You see? I appoint you hour-watcher and hemerologist. Daylight saving does so mix one up."

Torquil's tall figure was silhouetted for a moment in front of a window, but the doctor went straight on.

"As I say, my dears, it is a disappointment. Perhaps they will come. At least Lucy—I feel certain she will come. Why, it will be wonderful! What's that, sir? High over head? Scarcely the reading of a sailorman. Nor of one versed in the stars, eh, Jamshid? But it will do. Indeed, it bids us hurry. I fear I must change my clothing." I could imagine him looking down at his soiled dress shirt.

"You will wait for me here. Yes, yes—you too, Mr. Torquil. You will not want to miss what is in store for us. I think I can promise you a sight, an experience you will never forget— never, sir, this side the grave!" He was waxing oratorical, his nervous eloquence an index of excitement. "Come, Jamshid. Though you, I know, will not participate, for me it must be full regalia—the white linen tonight. You may lay it out while I perform my ablutions."

Then, to the others: "I shall return shortly to escort you to the House of Life."

It was a weird hour for a bath, I thought, but if Dr. Sarx felt the need of one, he had doubtless earned it. I wondered how long he would be and whether I had better use my whistle. I decided on a brief preliminary move. Before I hid myself in the lab, I would give these good people a word of encouragement.

Mrs. Budding was arguing in a low tone with Mr. Torquil. I could scarcely make out what she said.

"Francis, I wish you'd go home. I'll be perfectly safe. And heaven knows what kind of rigmarole he's planning. Why don't you run along? We'll be all right, won't we, Warburton?"

One thing struck me as strange. From the anxiety of a few moments ago, she seemed now to have forgotten all about Lucy. Her protest to the doctor had sounded genuine enough; now she seemed as confident of her daughter's safety as if she knew exactly where she was. But I was intent on offering further reassurance.

Silently, I crept around the outside of a light patch. Dropping to my hands and knees, I made my way against the house wall till I knelt beside the nearest window. I spoke with my face close to the ground—an old trick to disguise the place of origin.

"Don't worry about Lucy," I said. "She's perfectly all right." And indeed I thought she was.

But even as I spoke, there was a sound of sudden movement in the room; I heard Mrs. Budding gasp; and Mr. Torquil said, "Why, hello, Lucy. We were just talking about you."

Warburton was less casual. "Lucy, you dimwit! Couldn't you stay out of this? I'm just about to find out—"

"—what I want to find out, too." Lucy's voice was firm. "I'm glad you're all right, Warburton."

"Thank you." The boy addressed himself to his mother. "I think, before Cutty comes back, we ought to get Lucy out of here. She could stay with Charlie Vickers till this—this performance is over."

"Charlie's probably sound asleep," said Mrs. Budding.

"Oh no, he isn't," Lucy contradicted. "He's outside. I just ran away from him."

Blast the girl! I thought I had taken every precaution to keep her away from the party. It had never occurred to me that she would cross up Charlie—and me, too.

"I've just as much right as anyone else to be here," Lucy said, "in spite of all efforts to keep me under wraps. Under wraps is right! Bags over the head—here in my own house! You have no monopoly, Warburton—"

"Oh, shut up," said Warburton. "Here he comes."

If the doctor was returning, it was time for me to be about my business.

As quickly and as silently as possible, I returned to the outer fringe of darkness. Cover gained, I took out my whistle and blew twice. It was a crow call, and it sounded very peculiar indeed in the quiet night. If no one else deemed the evening an odd one, the local colony of rooks must certainly have thought so.

Having duly startled the birds, I sped around the corner of the house, gained the breezeway, and entered by the main back door. To my immediate right, an ell led off the hall to the laboratory. I realized that I was standing exactly where the visiting casket had been stored.

As my father had promised, the lab door was unlocked. I pushed it open into darkness and started across the forbidden room, hands outstretched to guard against the metal table. On this object, however, I managed to bark my shins once more before I reached the farther wall. I brought up at last—as nearly as I could tell—at just about the spot from which I had watched Jamshid. It was here, I remembered, that I had reached up and felt—as I thought at the time—a low ceiling. Stretching myself again, I touched the same steely surface; but I realized now that it was the underside of a gallery.

The corner to my right sheltered no stairway—that much I knew. Accordingly, I inched to the left where, sure enough, my hand caught the outthrust curve of a metal guardrail. And though the centripetal steps were tiny, I managed to mince my way up. With any light, I told myself, my perch would command the entire room below; and on the floor of this platform, I crouched, making myself as small as possible and waiting for something to happen.

I had not to wait long.

After no more than two or three minutes, the laboratory door, which I had carefully shut behind me, opened. In its light, I saw one of the dark assistants, his appearance quite transformed by a change of costume. Instead of the usual houseman's outfit, Butrus (or Ali—I wasn't sure which) now wore a loincloth of light color, sandals, and nothing else. The loincloth, in the fashion of hieroglyphic characters, was folded around his waist with a longer panel pendent at the center. I was reminded of the sporran with which Scotsmen adorn their kilt.

But there was nothing of the Scottish claymore in the sword that this warrior carried. Sharply curved as it was, I took it to be a *khepesh*, the weapon that the Nile gods give to a king as a pledge of victory. Its blade would be of bronze, and if I remembered correctly, it would date from the Twelfth Dynasty. For entertainment's sake, I wondered what the average Cape Codder would make of this outfit.

The man pressed a switch near the door, and light slowly flooded the lower portion of the room. I say the lower portion, for the fixtures were recessed halfway up the walls and slanted downward—some from the underside of my private balcony —for all the world like the illumination of an operating theater. I mention this detail because it left my perch in deeper shade than ever. This fact subsequently proved to be important.

For the first time, I had a real look at the piece of furniture on which I had been bound the night before. It was indeed of metal and porcelain with black upholstered cushioning—a cross between an operating table and a dentist's chair. Jointed in several places, it was controlled, apparently, by foot pedals; plumbing was handy by; and a white-topped folding shelf sprang from one arm.

For the rest, the room was rather as I had pictured it—cold, clean, and clinical. A double rank of metal drawers, each with its shining pulls, climbed up the wall beside the door. To the left, a benchlike *mastaba* afforded the only seating. But to my right, between the drawers and my hiding place, three statues, larger than life, had been stationed like so many easy chairs. These were the transfers from the studio, readily recognizable as Mrs. Budding (seated in the middle) and the children, one on either side. Somehow or other, the doctor had found time since morning to complete the coloring of Mrs. Budding's image. It could not be said that the tints were lifelike, but feature for feature, the face was hers; however unreal, the colors were those of her morning make-up. Down the front of each figure, from head to toe, ran a sinister incision, and I realized that somewhere at the back there was a corresponding hinge.

The second assistant entered, dressed like the first. At once the two men busied themselves with minor chores, dusting the drawer pulls, moving the chairlike table from the center of the room to the side directly underneath me, flicking a soft cloth lightly over the carven features of the mother and her children. Helping himself from a shallow built-in cabinet, one of the busy pair laid out beside the table several instruments, a bottle of dark fluid, and what looked like a hypodermic syringe.

"All set for the Mad Scientist," I told myself, remembering the many movies I had seen of gurgling retorts and flashing gauges. The trouble was, the jest was too uncomfortably near the truth; and I, who had always laughed with scorn at the clicks and bubbles of cinematic alchemists, was now involved up to my neck in the very same sort of thing. "No trap doors," I assured myself—but I wasn't even sure of that.

The door to the hall opened again, admitting the doctor. He was doing his best to live up to my apprehensions, for in the place of his dinner clothes (or the multicolored *jallabiyah* of breakfast time), he wore a long white robe tucked up with a belt of the same material. Most remarkable of all, he had removed what I now realized must have been a wig; he was not bald—he was positively bare—and the top of his head shone like a pink obscenity under the lights.

From some dim recess of mind, I remembered that the First and Second Priests of Amen were required to be shaven, shorn, and plucked. The good doctor had hedged: his eyebrows and mustache were still grotesquely in place. In his hand he carried what appeared to be a scroll.

As befits a host, this vision waved his guests into the room —Mrs. Budding first, then Warburton and Lucy, finally Francis Torquil. The two children looked as if they were shivering. The doctor's voice was oddly resonant in the bleak room as he invited the others to seat themselves on the *mastaba*. "Welcome," he said, "to the House of Life."

The door was shut. Butrus and Ali, splendid figures both, stood on each side of it.

"It is fitting and also needful," said the doctor, "that I begin the event of this evening with prayer. The words I say, you may not understand, but the purpose and the meaning of my speech will become clear. We are on the verge, you and I, of an unparalleled experience—one for which I have taken long years to prepare. None of you is here by accident; each of you has his part to play. You may be well assured that the ancients whom I follow knew more than later men concerning life and death. They knew that the dead may be served by the inanimate, the fallen hero by his image. To this end they made for each hero his *ushabti* (which is in the older tongue *shawabti*) to do his corvée duties. For each dead man, there was the corresponding statue; and while the mummy slept, the image labored through the nighttime."

I can't say that I was fascinated by this talk. It was too long and too pontifical and overconfident that we were all of us as nutty about Egypt as the speaker. The last thing I wanted in the early-pearly morning was a lecture on the valley of the Nile. Besides—it might have been my imagination—but it seemed to me that in the doctor's speech there was an element of threat. I stayed where I was, however, remembering my father's order: "Don't do anything else till you hear from me."

"It was realized," the doctor went on, "that special powers to control and to command lay with the mummy, for he was, so to say, the very Person, the real Self, the actual Body of the dead." (You could *hear* the capital letters.) "Except," said the doctor, coughing slightly, "for those portions of the body carefully removed for storage in canopic jars. What was *not* realized, nor attempted, was the union of the Person and the Image, the combination of Body and Statue—with the strength of both in one. Nor did the ancients venture to experiment with families, between whose members, properly prepared, such power must be greatly magnified."

His voice dropped to a whisper. "I think," he said, "they were afraid." Then, in more normal tones: "And now, with your permission, I go to my prayers."

I saw one of the guardsmen move, and the lights in the laboratory dimmed. The doctor turned and faced the wall of drawers; he knelt, his arms at first outstretched, then folded on his chest; and there issued from him, in a foreign voice, a foreign tongue.

I know a smattering of several languages—as well as some Levantine dialects—but I had never heard the one in which he prayed. It wasn't Arabic or any of the commoner derivatives. Nor did it have the ringing consonantal impact of the Coptic mass. (I have long since come to the conclusion that it was a form of demotic, the language that came into general use along the Nile some seven centuries before Christ.) But there was about it a metallic quality that seemed to suit the room.

The prayer ceased, or at least the vocal part of it. Dr. Sarx remained on his knees, and it seemed to me the lights came up a little. Then, without audible bidding, the two assistants left their place beside the door and advanced on the wall of drawers. Each man seized a handle at convenient height, and one of the receptacles—it was a topless casket—slid on invisible and silent rollers to project beyond the others and reveal its contents.

At least the contents was revealed to *me* in my eyrie. How much the others saw, I cannot say; but I heard an indrawn breath that may have come from Mrs. Budding—for in the casket-drawer there lay a mummy, wondrously preserved. The face, the color of scorched paper, stretched across strong bones. The eyes were covered with colored gems. A *djed*-pillar (the fetish of Ptah) adorned the beaded collar. The exterior garment was of royal blue. From the usual abdominal incision, a silver *udjat*-eye peered at the fingers of the folded hands, hooded in stalls of gold. The age of the dead man it was impossible to fix. Dr. Sarx was right about one thing: there was a Presence among us; we, the observers, were ourselves observed.

'Almost immediately, the doctor opened his scroll and placed it before him. Now he stood and gazed full on the mummy in the open drawer. Looking over his shoulder, as it were, I saw from my balcony that he had spread on a small wooden frame the linen likeness of a god. I took it to be Osiris, the symbolic lord of resurrection, and from what followed, I was proven right.

The doctor beckoned to the nearer guardsman, took something from him, and proceeded to scatter what looked like earth over the surface of the picture. Another supply—another sprinkling. Seed, I thought, recalling something of the rite that I had read. Then water—from a little pitcher handed him. Next thing, I knew, the barley grains would sprout.

But it was not the magic sprouting of a plant that caught my breath. It was the movement—just a stirring first—of the still shape within the open drawer.

Just a stirring at first and then a notable upheaval of the wrappings—layer upon layer, one supposed—and a rising of the upper portion of the body. The torso asserted itself with astonishing smoothness—not in the jerky movements to be expected of an ancient mechanism but by a single lubricated surge. Upright the mummy sat and, in the same weird, flowing fashion, turned its head toward us—as if the sightless eyes could penetrate their coverings. There was no stirring of the gold-tipped hands. These remained folded on the creature's breast.

Reason told me it was a trick. Like the sprouting plant I had expected to see, this spectacle of resurrection *could* be faked—that I knew. We who watched might even be the subjects of mass hypnotism, that amazing technique by which Indian magicians can induce in numbers of people at once the same hallucination. But in this instance, reason could argue all night—to no effect. Dr. Sarx himself was the most telling argument against a trick, for at the sight of the moving mummy, the doctor was transfixed past any possible pretense, his back as rigid as if strung on wire, his body taut with an ungovernable tension. If anyone in that extraordinary chamber was appalled, dumfounded, and—I think—dismayed, that person was Caspar Sarx.

But gradually the fear went from him. Somehow he came to know that having done this thing—having effected this miracle in the open casket—he was himself the mummy's master. Pride visibly replaced his terror. Under the long white robe, his pulpy body gained a semblance of authority. Turning toward the rest of us, he spread his arms out—in the gesture of a showman.

"The witness of the dead!" he cried. "The witness of the dead!"

I must admit that the whole business jarred me nastily, and I clung with desperation to the skirts of common sense. The guardsmen were prostrate on the floor. Mrs. Budding stared in trancelike immobility. Mr. Torquil appeared fiercely angry. The children had risen and stood in front of the *mastaba,* utterly involved. It was no place—and no scene—in my opinion, for children.

But the doctor had decided it was time to make a speech.

"To you, my friends, vast honor has been done. And to me, the humble agent of this wonder, great grace has been shown. He who was once among us has awakened. It is his wish to see the consummation of my dream—the union of the Body and the Image."

Now the capitals were unmistakable. "Three of you, near and dear to him, will serve at his desire. Three of you, knit by ties of blood, will give your lives into the keeping of your image.

"Elizabeth Budding—to the preparation table!"

Horrified, I saw the children's mother rise and start toward the doctor. Instantly, Torquil was beside her, and his voice rang out in protest.

"I don't know what you're planning, Sarx, but Mrs. Budding will have no part in it. I don't like your magic or whatever you call it, and I don't believe in your tricks. We've had enough of this. We're leaving." His announcement embraced the children.

But the two assistants were on their feet, bronze blades flashing in their hands. Disregarding them completely, Mrs. B. broke away from Torquil's restraining grip and headed for the doctor like a dedicated sleepwalker.

Francis Torquil sounded almost like a husband. "I will not have it," he insisted. "Liz, for the children's sake—"

But words would not stop her. At a gesture from the doctor, she approached the operating table.

The fat man barked at Torquil. "You, sir, desist. Nothing will affect Mrs. Budding save such action as she takes herself."

And *that's* not much of a guarantee, I thought.

"Make yourself comfortable on the table, my dear." The doctor's voice was oily. Torquil stepped forward, hands balled into fists. The guardsmen did not move. Away from Torquil, toward the sinister chaise longue, the doctor kept his distance. Then, from the folds of his robe, he pulled a long-barreled automatic. The thin snout and wooden butt suggested a Luger.

"It was not my intention," he said, "to introduce the inappropriate. Stand back—back against the *mastaba,* all of you."

"All of you" meant Mr. Torquil and the children, for the guards were motionless and Mrs. Budding paid no more attention to the doctor than he did to her. She was standing by what he had called the "preparation table," idly fingering the objects on its porcelain wing.

"First," said the doctor, "I will show you the places of destiny." He grunted an order in Arabic, and the two assistants— rather reluctantly, I thought—moved toward the three statues. At a further word from their master, they hooked their fingers in the frontal crack of the middle figure, pulling the sides apart till the opening gaped wide. In the same ghastly way each of the children's images was parted.

"There!" said Dr. Sarx, and now he turned to Mrs. Budding. "There is a home and rest and peace and power for each of you! Are you not glad to see? While the lamented lord looks on?" He waved at the upright mummy.

"He watches with his ageless eyes," pronounced the doctor. "And for you, there is only the Gateway—a pleasant one, my dear. Sit, if you will, just here. Lie back at ease. 'Yet a little sleep, a little slumber, a little folding of the hands to sleep'— how does it go? Here is the instrument."

I suppose that each of us by now who had heard him speak was literally numb. It was not the doctor's Luger that restrained us. If the others felt what I did, it was freezing fascination and a desperate faith that somebody was sure to *do* something—before it was too late, before the nightmare became fact.

He had moved to the head of the table couch and stood so nearly beneath the edge of my balcony that I had to crane my neck to keep him visible. I saw his free hand grasp the hypodermic.

"It is permitted that you give yourself this joy," he said. "See, I will show you."

"Not tonight, you won't!" It was my father's voice, bursting across the room from the wall of drawers. "O.K., Jonathan! Charge!"

I vaulted the railing and dropped like a stone on the doctor's head. As his body crumpled under me, I blessed the rolls of fat that broke my fall and kicked at his gun hand. Someone screamed—it may have been Lucy—and the doctor, nowise stunned, reared up beneath my weight like a Brahma bull. Furiously, I clung to him with arms and legs; in hands like hams, he seized my wrists and tried to pull me over his bucking back. I heard my father shouting—presumably to Torquil—"Don't shoot, man! Wait for me!" I guessed that Torquil had the gun, that the spell was broken and the gods of the Nile would go hungry. There was a gibbering of Arabic from the guardsmen and the patter of their naked feet. Both of them, swords forgotten, gained the door and opened it. Over a heaving shoulder, I could see them turn the corner of the hall.

In a sudden explosion of strength, the doctor rose to his feet, lifting me with him. Tottering for one uncertain step under his burden, he threw himself backward directly on top of me, his great rear end descending like a maul on my defenseless stomach.

He broke free then, and a shot rang out. Gasping for breath, I raised myself in time to see the doctor's vast white bulk speed for the exit.

"Stop him, somebody!" my father yelled, and even as he spoke, a small, swift shape had lanced across the room, grabbed at the doctor's robe, and Lucy—running, half-dragged, half-carried at his heels—went out through the door that slammed behind them both.

Chapter

24

Looking back on the incident, it hardly seems reasonable that my sudden arrival on the scene should have so disrupted the party. My father admitted afterward that we had run it pretty close with Mrs. Budding's hypodermic. On the other hand, his action as the levitated mummy had pretty well shattered the assistants, and surprise—as much as my performance—had taken care of Dr. Sarx.

For the moment, that is. In point of fact, the doctor was off and away with his servants and, what was worse, with Lucy.

But as I looked around the room—despite the gravity of our circumstance—I burst out laughing. The mummy had swung himself out of his berth, no doubt expecting to join the fray. Mask torn off and beard gone with it, my father's face appeared above the gaudy cerements like an anachronism in astonishment. He was just that, poor man—completely trammeled by the lower portion of his wrappings. Like a boy in a sack, he was fighting one leg against the other, striving desperately to free himself and reeling off a string of curses in Swahili.

Pistol in hand, Francis Torquil ran past us both to the door. The big spring lock had functioned. Warburton was pulling and turning the knob—but to no avail. Mrs. Bud-

ding, rather surprisingly, was sitting upright on her "preparation table," issuing orders with more emotion than I had
thought her capable of.

"Get that door open, you idiots! Lucy's out there with that
lunatic! Don't you see? He's got himself a hostage! Major
Flower, will you kindly step out of that petticoat and organize
these people?" She ceased firing for a moment, looked briefly
at me, and said, "That was a brave leap, Posy. I was afraid
nothing was ever going to happen."

"Talk about bravery," said Mr. Torquil. "You were the
brave one, Liz." He left the door and moved to her side. "To
lie there defenseless—"

"I wouldn't have been defenseless once he'd handed me the
needle. All I had to do was turn it on him." I had given her
far too little credit. "Why not use the gun on the lock?" she
asked.

"Exactly what we'll do." My father was mobile again, free
of his funerary swathings, an odd sight now in mummy top
and bathing trunks. As I lay still winded on the floor, I could
imagine his fury and mortification, for the role he likes to
play is that of *deus ex machina* —without a flaw.

Now, as if to make up for some delinquency, he broke into
action.

"Let me have the gun a minute, Torquil. Wonderful performance, Mrs. Budding."

At the first blast, the door shivered, but the lock held.

"Shame to wreck this hardware"—and he fired again. This
time the heavy shell performed as ordered, and the next
moment we were all of us crowding the doorway. I didn't feel
very lively, but I could navigate.

"The Egyptians turned toward the front of the house," I
said. "I couldn't see where Sarx and Lucy went."

"In that case," said my father, "you can go out the back.
Alert your friend Charlie Vickers. Warburton can go with

you, I guess." He didn't look at Mrs. Budding. "The rest of us'll search the house. Sarx can't have gotten far. And Jamshid's somewhere around. Cars taken care of, Posy? Good. Mrs. Budding, you'd better stay with us."

As I didn't think that Torquil would go without her, this last edict seemed a bit superfluous. Nor did I understand why my father felt it necessary to go back and shut the casket drawer from which he had made his appearance. At any rate, our pursuit squad parted in the hall.

The brougham, I thought, as the only car immediately movable, needed protection. Charlie Vickers had been told to watch beside it—after making fast the other automobiles. But Charlie Vickers had also been told to hang onto Lucy—with regrettable results.

I hustled Warburton around the dark shape of the studio to the spot where the electric buggy had been left. It wasn't there.

Instead, the moon shone down on the figure of a man, stretched at full length on the ground—almost precisely where the car had been. It was Charlie Vickers! Our chariot was stolen, and our watchman had had it. As I bent over the chauffeur to check the extent of his damage, a quiet voice hailed us from the bushes.

"Wabbit'n! Posy!" Mr. Snow emerged from concealment. "Heard you comin'," he said. "Didn't know who it was. Glad it's you. Terrible things goin' on." He took off his droopy hat and mopped his brow.

"I got here just in time to see it happen. Back in the bushes, I was. Charlie was standin' here—'longside the little car. Mindin' his own business, Charlie was, and lookin' at the moon. I was just about to speak to him when that doctor feller arrives from over by the house. All dressed up in a sheet, he was—and before you c'd say Jack Robinson, he hits Charlie in the neck with the side of his hand like a chopper. Charlie makes a noise like a sea robin, and down goes Charlie." Mr. Snow looked ruefully at the victim. "Nice feller, too—Charlie."

"Then what?" I asked, trying to find Charlie's pulse.

"Then the doctor feller jumps in the broome"—Mr. Snow pronounced it like the first lord of that ilk—"and away he goes."

I gave a sigh of relief. There was a pulse all right, and Charlie was stirring like a boxer after a long, long count. But what cheered me most was Mr. Snow's most notable omission.

"And you didn't see anything of Lucy?" It was more of a stated reassurance than a question. The reply was not what I expected.

"Eyyup," said Mr. Snow. (It was his usual way of saying "yes.") "Eyyup. Seen Lucy, too. Came from the same direction as Sarkuss did. She seen him hit Charlie—must of. But Sarkuss didn't see her." He chuckled with satisfaction.

"Well, where is she now?" I demanded.

"She went with him." He chuckled again. "He don't know it, but she went with him."

"How?" Warburton wanted to know. (I did, too.)

"Oh, she climbed up behind," said Mr. Snow. "Know that little rumble, sticks out th'end of the broome—like a bustle, sort of? Well, soon's Lucy seen the doctor feller get in the car, she climbs up on that there shelf. Didn't like it, though." He paused meditatively.

"What do you mean—she didn't like it?"

"Couldn't of, 'cause last I seen of her, she was on the roof."

"Good show," said Warburton devoutly.

As for me, I could picture my young friend insecurely perched on the belvedere of that ancient vehicle, larruping through the countryside with a wilder driver than even Mrs. Little.

"Which way did they go?" I asked. (This thing was getting more and more like a rerun Western.)

A voice from the ground answered me.

"Only way they could go—down the trail to the beach. After Lucy gave me the slip, I blocked the drive with the Cadillac." Charlie's contribution ended in a groan. "Doggone that beer-bellied Buddha—he near to broke my neck."

To the best of my recollection, the brougham had not required a highway: it was perfectly possible that the doctor —and his outside passenger—were off on a route of their own devising. But I judged the trail to the beach to be likeliest, at least until we had manpower enough for a spread-out search.

"Warburton," I told him, "you run back to the house and report our news. Tell my father we're heading for the water, and we'll post somebody at Mr. Snow's—er—shanty."

The boy looked at me in silence.

"What's the matter with *you?*" I asked.

"Your father!" he exploded. "Who's your father?" Then light began to dawn. "Do you mean to say the Gnome is your father?"

I'd forgotten he didn't know. "He is indeed," I said.

"How absolutely weird and wonderful!" Warburton appeared delighted. "I'm sorry—go on. I'm to tell the Gnome— your father, that is—that we'll be down at the shore. What else?"

"You can tell him that the drive is blocked and remind him that Charlie has all the car keys. I hardly think the doctor'll circle back. And ask him for orders. I'll give you two minutes; then Mr. Snow and I'll start for the beach. Charlie, if you can move, you'd better go in with Warburton. You're in no shape for a hike."

Charlie had managed, with Mr. Snow's help, to get to his feet.

"It's a fact I don't feel up to much," he admitted. "Doggone that horse doctor!" His hand went to his neck as he limped after our messenger.

"Bit of a blow comin' on," said Mr. Snow, looking skyward. Clouds were threatening the moon.

"I hope Lucy doesn't fall off that roof," I said.

Chapter

25

Warburton caught up with us some hundred yards along the trail, and I remembered my first walk with him down the same route—was it months or years before?

"They nabbed Ali," said Warburton, "but Butrus apparently's gotten away. The phones are out of whack, and my mother's taking the Cadillac down to the village to get the policeman."

Mr. Snow snorted. "Pibbidy? Pibbidy'll be so sound asleep, she'll have to carry him back."

"Mr. Torquil's going with her, I suppose?"

"No," said Warburton. "She said she'd rather go alone. She insisted on going. I think she's so worried about Lucy that she just wants something to do without waiting around."

"What about Jamshid?" I asked.

"Oh, he's there all right. He never heard a thing. From the time he left us in the living room, he claims there wasn't a sound. I think perhaps he helped catch Ali, though. They've never liked each other very much. He's going to stay at the house, so somebody'll be there till Munce gets back—Jamshid is, I mean. Mr. Torquil and your father will probably follow us. When I left, they were trying to get Charlie Vickers to go to bed. He said he didn't want to miss anything. . . . Gosh, it's getting cold!"

It was indeed a cold breeze that hit our faces and stirred the undergrowth on either side of the sunken track. Mr. Snow and I stuck to the sandy ruts while Warburton showed a preference for the grass-grown center strip. With more and more clouds creeping over the moon, it grew harder to find sure footing: even Mr. Snow—who must have known the way by heart—stumbled twice and advised caution.

"May's well take it easy, Posy. Ain't no place for Sarkuss to go 'cept along the beach. Provided he started this way—and I'll swear he did—he wouldn't do much turnin' off." The banks rose steeply on each side, heavily overgrown with bay and pine. "Besides, we're expectin' reinforcements." He looked back over his shoulder, but behind us there was only solid dark. All we could hear was the rising wind and, somewhere on ahead, the growing protest of the water.

The moon was now almost totally obscured, and it was with a sense of some relief that I felt the trail slope downward and knew we were entering on its last sweeping curve to the beach. There was marsh to our right, and as none of us wanted a plunge in reedy mud, we slowed our pace.

"Beware," said Warburton in a rather foolish voice. "Beware the 'haunts of coot and hern.' " The place seemed to stir his memories of Tennyson, and I felt that I could do without them.

What light there was showed Mr. Snow's establishment against the dull gleam of the bay; the sand itself was a strip of paleness, as far as we could see quite uninhabited. For a moment we stood under the last bluff headland where, sheltered from the wind, we could command a broad view of the beach.

It was here that we were greeted by a voice from over our heads.

"This is where I jumped off," said Lucy, "here by the battery. My, but you guys took your time." She was speaking from the thicket just above us. I was so relieved to hear her that I asked no questions. "He drove the car," she said, "smack into the water. You can't see it from here, but it's right beyond Mr. Snow's boathouse."

"Where'd he go himself?" It was my father asking. He had slipped up quietly behind us, Mr. Torquil at his side. The clan was gathering.

"Up the beach toward Littles' Cove," said Lucy. "I think he's looking for the pram."

"For the pram?" Warburton sounded skeptical. "What's he going to do—row to Boston?"

"He won't find it," I said. "I looked there this—yesterday morning."

"But you didn't look this afternoon," said Mr. Snow mysteriously. "See there!"

The moon broke through the overcast, and a silver track unrolled across the bay. Into this swathe of light, the squat shape of the pram moved out from the high reeds surrounding Littles' Cove. Two men weighed down the boat, one at the oars, the other low on the stern thwart.

"View hulloa!" cried Lucy from her perch above us. "It's Cutty all right, and he's got Butrus with him."

Without a further word to urge us, we moved off in a pack along the final stretch to the beach. Only Warburton hung back, and I heard him call to Lucy. His voice was very small against the wind, and so was hers as she answered him:

"I'm staying here. I've got my reasons. Why don't you stay, too?"

Apparently, the invitation appealed to him, for when last seen, young Warburton was scaling the overhung front of the headland. As I looked back, I was reminded that the second story of Dr. Sarx's house commanded a splendid view of the water, for from the shore we could see the upstairs lights of Sexton's Prim shining into the night.

Ahead of us, beyond the shanty, Mrs. Little's brougham sat in a foot of restless water—for all the world, as my father remarked, "like a bathing-machine at Brighton." At his bidding, we lined up close beside the fishing shack.

The pram was making toward us and keeping close in. I guessed that the doctor was unaware of our pursuit. Where he had picked up Butrus was anyone's conjecture.

My father was in consultation with Mr. Snow. The latter shook his head. "Better get them to come in," the old salt said. "Water's too choppy for that there pram." (You'd have thought his chief concern was for the safety of our quarry.) "Nothin' here we can launch. Two-three motors in the boathouse, but where we goin' to put them?"

My father had apparently made up his mind. "Sarx!" he called, and his voice carried above the weather. "Sarx! Come in out of that! We've got you covered."

An indistinguishable roar of words came from the pram. I thought I made out reference to a "blasphemer." There were gestures from the fat man, and his square-ended craft began to veer away from the beach. She was making heavy going in the chop, and I could easily imagine how hard she was to steer.

"Bring that boat in or we fire!" But my father was bluffing, for no gun was in his hand.

And this time, instead of by words, he was answered by bullets. Three times in quick succession a flash and a crack came from the laboring rowboat—gunplay by guesswork, doubtless, but the third shot plowed up sand six feet away from me.

"The nasty feller's got a spare rod. Get behind those rocks, boys." My father tried another hail. "Come back, Sarx! You'll drown in that tub!"

"He's heading for *Bluejacket*," said Mr. Snow. "See where

she's moored?" A white shape tossed under the fitful moon some hundred yards from shore. Toward that white shape, the overburdened pram made its precarious way.

Another shot, and something rattled through the lobster pots.

"Could we swim after him?" I asked. (I admit it was one of my stupider questions.)

"And be potted in the water? Or whacked over the head with an oar? Not tonight, Posy. Use your brain, sonny boy."

I was trying to, but it didn't help.

"If he makes it to *Bluejacket*, what then, Mr. Snow?" It was Francis Torquil asking.

"Why then he's master of some sixteen feet o' dory and seven-and-a-half good horses."

"You don't mean," I protested, "that he'd take *Bluejacket* to sea?" I had visions of the doctor on the broad Atlantic.

"Matter of fact, she's right good in a seaway. But he won't have to take her that far. *Queen o' Sheba*'s anchored in the lee o' th'island. Saw her myself this morning."

"*Queen of Sheba?*"

"Sarkuss's cruiser. I told you 'bout her. Big boat. Big engine. He can run her to Bermuda if he likes."

My father groaned, for all the while we talked, the pram with its galley slave and pistol-packing cox was drawing nearer to *Bluejacket* and farther from our grasp. If ever four people knew frustration, we were they—our quarry vanishing before our eyes, and nothing, absolutely nothing, at hand to do about it.

The wind kept up, but the moon grew brighter. Out at the mooring, we saw the pram come alongside the dory. The rowing stopped, and the big figure of the doctor rose, unsteady in the pitching boat. There was a lurching movement, and we saw that he had gotten himself successfully aboard the larger craft. Butrus had not made fast to the buoy but was apparently holding to *Bluejacket*'s gunwale.

The doctor moved to the bow, and I heard Mr. Snow's low chuckle.

"I wish him joy o' Wabbit'n's mousings," the old man said. "S'pose they'll set the pram adrift."

But however my young charge had left the lines, the doctor slipped his mooring quickly, and both the boats were free.

Surprisingly agile for so big a man, Dr. Sarx made his way astern in the now wallowing dory, and we saw him working on the engine cover. Fascinated and furious, we watched his final preparation for escape.

It was at this moment that Butrus chose to make his move. Whether it was because he was weary of hanging on to the bigger boat or perhaps afraid that he might lose his grip, we saw him rise to a crouch, and then—for the stride across both gunwales—gain his feet. Instantly, the doctor struck. An oar, snatched from the bottom of the dory, caught the Egyptian servant squarely in his middle. Driven outward and upward by the weapon, his body arched against the sky. With a wail that pierced the wind, he plunged into the bay.

What followed was almost too horrible to watch. From where we were, we could not see the man in the water. But three times we saw the doctor raise the oar above his head, and three times it came down sickeningly to bury its blade in a splash of white slaughter. Then the doctor returned to the needs of his engine.

None of us could voice what he felt. Close to being sick, I remembered some little boys I had once known in Hanover who caught mice alive in wire traps, turned them loose in deep water, and pelted the swimming creatures with stones until they died.

And it was as we stood there, filled with disgust and a hatred of our own sheer impotence, that suddenly there was a flash of light across the beach; from behind us there sounded the booming crash of an artillery piece fired at close range. Something went whining through the air over our heads, and an acrid cloud of smoke closed in around us. Almost at once, there came a second flash and the sound of a second explosion. Again the scream of flying shot, and again the cloud of smoke.

Then silence.

Chapter

26

The smoke began to clear away, driven in swirling eddies by the wind. It was much as if the moonlight etched a pattern on the fringes of our darkness.

Footsteps sounded behind us. It was the children, on the run.

"Did we get him?" asked Warburton. No one else had spoken since the doctor used his oar. The air grew clearer, and to seaward we made out the buoy, a white blob in dark water. Some feet from it floated the pale belly of an upturned boat: *Bluejacket* had capsized. However hard we looked, there was no more to see.

Except, that is, the empty pram, adrift halfway to shore.

"Tide's makin'," said Mr. Snow—and it was as if he were talking to himself. "Those there boats'll wash ashore. Lots o' things wash ashore if the tide's right."

I was already stripping off my shirt.

"What's on your mind, son?" My father knew, but he asked anyway.

"Somebody's got to look for those men," I said. "That man Butrus—"

"He'll never be able to swim," someone offered, "not after those blows on the head."

No one mentioned the doctor. Nor was I looking forward with any great joy to encountering either of our recent enemies, particularly if deranged—by injury or otherwise. But something had to be done, and water, fortunately, is one thing I'm not afraid of.

Mr. Snow began to make negative noises, but my father reassured him with a few words about my luck in the Junior Olympics. "Besides," he said, "I'm going, too—at least as far as the pram." He began to peel off the upper garments of the mummy. "Warburton," he asked, through several layers of clothing, "how in heaven's name did you and Lucy manage to hit the boat with those antiquities up there?" He got an arm free and gestured toward the bluff.

Lucy snatched the answer away from her brother. "Oh, we *knew* we had the range. We've practiced for months on the buoy—haven't we, Mr. Snow?"

" 'Fraid so," said the Ancient Mariner. " 'Fraid so."

"The question was," Lucy went on, "was it worth it to hurt *Bluejacket* in order to clobber Cutty? I said yes, but Warburton said no. That's why we delayed. But then when we saw what happened to poor Butrus, that settled it." She looked out at the bay. "I think we must have caught a gunwale and barreled her over."

"Can Sarx swim, do you know?" I asked.

"Oh, yes," said Warburton. "At least I think so. He always talked a lot about swimming. And I doubt if we got him directly—not with our fix on the buoy. He was in the stern, remember—as far away from the buoy as he could be."

It was anything but reassuring to suppose that a lethal maniac lurked in the waters near the boat. But somebody had to find out.

My father and I waded a few feet, then slipped into the water. It felt like ice.

I headed straight for the capsized *Bluejacket*. Between the tops of nasty little seas, I caught an intermittent glimpse of her, stern down, weighted by the outboard. There was really nothing difficult about the swim, but the wind kept whipping up the wave crests in such a way as to discourage any more looking than was necessary to fix a course.

For some distance we stayed beside each other, almost stroke for stroke. Halfway out, my father veered off in the direction of the pram. Both boats were drifting—up and shoreward with the tide—so that the sea both helped and hindered swimmers toward them.

I took the last eight strokes at a breath and raised my head to find the dory just beyond me. It was my plan to circle the boat two or three times, seeking for signs of Butrus or his master. First, however, I dove under the upturned craft on the faint chance that one of them was pinned—or hiding—in the tunnel of the hull. As a matter of fact, there was breathing room—particularly in the bow, where splintered wood and a hole open to the sky marked the hit by round shot. Here a determined fugitive might conceivably have taken temporary shelter, but my groping in the darkness met with nothing but wet planks and some assorted minor flotsam bobbing on its private sea.

I dove again and came up outside the dory. The salt stung my eyes as I started around the almost submerged stern. And then I saw what I was looking for: against the white rise of the hull, a dark hand clutched with desperation at the meager purchase of a sheer strake and—even as I looked—lost hold and slipped away.

I lunged through the water and hit hard against a human body, already more than a foot below the surface. Though I tried to get my arms around him, his wet form slipped away, and I grasped at nothing in the dark. By daylight, it might have been possible to see the drowning man, but I had not even the help of the moon. *Bluejacket* lay directly between me and the silver path.

The only course was to dive again with the hope of an

encounter below the surface. I tried it once and succeeded only in cracking my head against the dory's gunwale on my way up.

I knew my chances were growing slimmer by the minute, but having seen that hand and touched that cold, wet flesh, I was determined to bring up someone—even if it turned out to be Dr. Sarx. Whichever of the men it was might well be wounded; the cheery thought occurred to me that sand sharks are attracted by the smell of blood. I had seen some specimens of *Odontaspis littoralis*—and in Cape Cod waters—whose company, under the circumstances, I could gladly do without.

Once more I took a deep breath of cold, wet air and kicked my heels up high behind me. At six feet down, I leveled off and crossed, as nearly as I could tell, directly under the dory. Precisely as I arched my back for reascent, something—some slippery substance of the deep—slid past my thigh. I flip-turned backward, and my hands grabbed hard at a mass of ropy fiber. For a moment, I thought I had hold of a sponge— or (shades of Sherlock!) a Portuguese man-of-war. But it was human hair, attached to a human body that seemed to resist my pull and exert a deliberate effort to keep us both in the depths.

I fought him as long as I could, actually fighting (as I was to learn) no more than his weight; but before we neared the surface, my chest was pounding and the bells were ringing in my ears. As we hit the air, I sucked too greedily and swallowed half a wave. But I managed to keep a firm grip on my catch; he offered no resistance, and I realized that he was unconscious. Keeping his head above water, I swiveled him around till I could see his face. It was—or had been—the face of Butrus. A great cut over one eye was oozing blood, and his jaw hung slack. How much water *he* had swallowed I could only imagine.

"Drag him over this way. I'm afraid to bring the boats too close together."

It was my father, calling from the pram. He sounded far away until I realized that he was shouting against the wind. Butrus simply would not float: if his feet rose a little, it was only to sink again almost at once. The best I could do was to keep his head back and his face up by my grip on his hair—and tread water in a kind of underwater waltz.

The pram was bouncing around like a ping-pong ball, and it took considerable work to get my free hand on its gunwale.

"He may be gone," said my father, "but we'd better heave him aboard." And by pushing and pulling from our respective positions, we managed to get him belly-down across a thwart, head and feet drooping to port and starboard of the little craft.

"How's the water?" my father asked. (He knew perfectly well what I thought of it.) "Any signs of the doctor?"

It hardly seemed the time to me for *conversazione*. Besides, I had no wind left for words.

But before I knew it, my father was in the water beside me.

"Time to trade," he said. There obviously wasn't room for three of us in the pram. "You hop in and give him artificial resp. I'll tow us home."

I didn't know whether I could make it, but I tried. And if you have ever climbed from a choppy sea into a crazy little flat-bottomed scow, already overloaded—and all on top of twenty minutes' submarine athletics—you have some notion of the shape I was in when I finally squatted in the forward cockpit.

Butrus was either dead or very close to it. As I struggled to rearrange him in the narrow limits of the boat, a quantity of water gushed from his mouth. I decided that prone resuscitation was in order: I could flop him over on his face and straddle him more easily than reach his mouth with mine. At first, however, there was no response at all to my manipulations.

I looked up once and saw the back of my father's head a

little beyond us. He had apparently made fast the painter of the pram somewhere about his person, for he was swimming strongly with both arms free. Dimly, I made out the shape of the shore; inland, faint pinkness glowed against the sky. It was frightfully cramped quarters—every time I pressed on Butrus's lungs, I took the chance of cracking his ribs.

The chop grew less boisterous, and I realized we were close to shore. A minute later and my father was wading hip-deep; the bottom of our bark scraped on sand; and a group of greeters, talking and gesticulating, gathered around us on the beach. It was a weird and shadowy spectacle, for the moon was more hidden than not; and we saw each other mostly by the pale reflected light that always lies on a body of water.

My father was a little out of puff as he gave orders.

"Help Posy with that fellow, will you? He needs to be worked on right away. If we pull it off, we'll want blankets and some way to get him back to the house."

"Here we are," announced a treble voice:

> " 'Strew on him rose-leaves lightly;
> Lap him in heady air—' "

"Heady air is just what he needs, Mrs. Little. Right now he's full of heady water. You *do* have blankets? Splendid. I could do with one myself."

There, sure enough, was the old lady—and Chicken Little by her side. Someone had gone off, said my erstwhile *chauffeuse*, with her brougham. She had felt she must find it. Chicken had insisted on accompanying her search.

"Have a ham sandwich," said Chicken, and actually produced a pack of them. Somehow those wonderful women had sensed a crisis at Sexton's Prim. On foot they had made it to the house, then down the trail to the beach.

"We spoke to Jamshid," Chicken explained. "He seemed awfully busy with those rags and things, but he told us where you'd gone. He's holding the fort."

I hadn't time for questions, and my mouth was full of sandwich.

With some irrelevance, Mrs. Little remarked:

> *"'Come one, come all! this rock shall fly*
> *From its firm base as soon as I!'"*

We believed her.

Then Lucy came up to me from somewhere and took hold of my hand. "You're cold, Posy," she said, "but you were very brave."

I started to look for my shirt. The air *was* cold, and a reaction to my recent exertions had set in. Meanwhile, Butrus had been laid on the sand, and Francis Torquil was giving him mouth-to-mouth treatment. Mr. Snow hovered above them, raising his head from time to time as if in invocation of the ancient sea gods.

"Some swimming," said Warburton. I hadn't realized he was standing next to me. "Did you see—you know—old Cutty?"

"No," I said, and as I spoke, there came a cheer from Torquil.

My father, draped in a blanket, reported from the casualty station: "He's breathing, right enough. Stick with it, Torquil!"

Lights swept the beach. A car crawled, jiggling and jouncing, down the curve beside the marsh. A driver must be brave, experienced, or both to ride those ruts in the dark. Mrs. Little's equipage had made it, to be sure, but Mrs. Little's equipage was sterner stuff than most.

"It's Pibbidy," said Mr. Snow. "Sure am surprised they managed to wake him up. Mrs. Budding did real good. Mornin', Pibbidy. You're out early. Mornin', Mrs. Budding."

"Hi, Munce," said Warburton. "Have a ham sandwich? Butrus was almost drowned, but Posy rescued him. Lucy and me fired the battery. How's Jamshid getting along?"

"Lucy and *I*," said Mrs. Budding. "We didn't go near the house. Mr. Peabody brought me by the shortcut from the Littles'. I called him from there. Then Mrs. Little insisted that I stay and wait while she and Chicken went exploring."

She looked over at Francis Torquil. He had stopped the artificial respiration and was wrapping Butrus in a blanket. "Hadn't we better get Butrus to the house?" His mistress was concerned.

At Mrs. Budding's question, my father, who had been in conversation with the village constable, raised his voice to all of us. "Mrs. Budding's right. We must get Butrus back to a warm bed. I'm afraid"—and his glance swept the white-capped water—"there's nothing more to do down here. Torquil, you and Posy get our friend into the car—Mr. Peabody's, I mean. I think it's safe to sit him up now—for that stretch. Mrs. Little, may I ask what you're doing?"

Unnoted by any of us, Chicken's grandmother had discreetly removed her shoes and stockings and was advancing with determination into the water. I had forgotten all about her vehicle, but she was making for the little brougham.

" '*Back and side go bare, go bare—*' "

So she sang, apparently referring to her feet.

"It just might work," my father murmured. "I doubt it, though. The tide's come up since Sarx did his parking. Those batteries are bound to be wet."

But we followed Mrs. Little, gathering around like curious beachcombers sniffing salvage. Officer Peabody kept clearing his throat. He had not yet been heard from and obviously felt his time had come.

"I'd like to know, please, who's in charge here."

Mrs. Little, who had mounted to the cabin, shouted out, "The lights won't work." I hadn't known that the car *had* any lights.

"Excuse me," said Officer Peabody. "Mrs. Budding told me

that there were arrests to be made. Will someone indicate—"

"She's never failed before!" It sounded as if Mrs. Little were going to cry.

"The batteries are wet," said Francis Torquil. "They must be."

Officer Peabody tried again: "I take it that Dr. Sarx is away?" Apparently, Mrs. Budding hadn't clued him in on much detail. "Will somebody—er, that is—will somebody please lay a complaint?"

"I will," said Mrs. Little. "My lovely, lovely car won't run." She was back on shore now. "Farewell, frail bark," she said, and then, apostrophizing the elements in general:

" 'Roll on, thou deep and dark blue Ocean, roll!' "

"Yes," said Officer Peabody. "And was it your plan to put this man here in my car?"

"Look!" cried Lucy (like a first-grade teacher). "Look!"

She was pointing back toward the trail and the lights of Sexton's Prim. We turned as if we were on spindles. In the distance, from behind the house, a bright red glow lit up the sky.

Chapter 27

I will say for the village constable that he acted with decision.

"Put that man in my car," he said, "and you two come along." He designated my father and me. (Lucy immediately grabbed my hand again, as if unwilling to face another separation.) "You, Mr. Snow, and this gentleman"—he indicated Francis Torquil—"will stay with the ladies and bring them up to the house as quickly as you can. I'm sorry, but it seems the best way. That glow can only mean one thing—and there's no fire engine nearer than Orleans. Have you a flashlight? No? Well, here's one. Now, if you'll fetch the passenger—"

The constable got into his car and started the business of turning around on the hard surface back of the shanty. We stuffed Butrus, blanket and all, into the back seat; and my father and I sat on each side of him, wedging him upright. He was breathing regularly now but seemed quite unaware of what was going on. Warburton we found already ensconced in front. Lucy promptly joined him, and as Officer P. made no demur, my father and I said nothing.

Our driver, as might have been expected, was a master of ruts, although he seemed not overly familiar with the pair that we were in. The Buick swayed and jounced and mounted small embankments and fell off again into sandy holes, but we made steady progress.

Where the trail cut into the headland, we lost sight of the sky; but as soon as we gained higher ground, our fiery objective became more and more apparent. The roof of the house appeared to be ablaze all over; until we turned left into the driveway proper, we could not see the lower floor for trees and planting; a hundred feet or so short of the porch, the whole strange picture burst upon us.

The house, or rather the back of the house, was serving as a chimney. There is no other way to describe it, for not a sign of fire showed across the front or at the side; the windows everywhere were dark—as if dark curtains had been drawn. Only from the roof—the roof that rose at the rear higher than anywhere else—flames flew up like banners, clouds of sparks exploded, and a vast column of rosy smoke mounted to the sky. The wind, as luck would have it, beat the blaze inshore, away from the rest of the house; and the fire appeared to be contained—as if its heart were in a great rectangular cauldron from which the lid had been burned off. Standing outside the vessel, what we saw was what rose up above its edges: the container itself was solid and dark, and all the night was filled with a noise of roaring.

"It's the lab!" my father shouted. "The fire's inside the lab —a concrete prism with a wooden roof! And oh, my word, the combustion in that furnace!"

So we stood watching—for there was nothing we could do except pray that the wind might hold and the fuel be exhausted.

Jamshid, I thought. Where was Jamshid who was to "hold the fort"? Warburton tugged at my sleeve.

"Mr. Peabody's going in," he said.

"He mustn't," said my father. "Where is he?"

"Round at the back," said Warburton. "Charlie Vickers is

there. He was sound asleep, and the noise woke him. He got out through his own back door."

"And Jamshid?" I asked. "Any sign of him?"

"My gosh! No. You don't think—"

"I don't know what to think," my father said. "What with a mummy-mad embalmer and a Parsi priest—"

"A *priest?*"

"Just that—with all the Parsi's loathing of preserved mortality. Come on, let's see if we can stop that fool policeman. Lucy—where's Lucy? Oh, there you are. Stick with us, Lucy girl. You've been on your own enough tonight."

I took a quick look in the car at our waterlogged passenger. He seemed to be asleep, and I followed the others around the west end of the house. Here there was enough expanse of lawn to catch the blowing sparks before they reached the trees; but the night air, cold as it had been at the beach, was actually hot with the breath of the fire. Even though the lower walls of the building were darkly undisturbed, they were impossible of close approach. Constable Peabody's project, as reported to us, would be suicide.

We were vastly relieved, then, as we crossed the breezeway —now a smoky tunnel—to come upon both Charlie and the officer. Oddly enough, they were paying no heed to the fire; indeed, their backs were turned to the burning building, and their whole attention was given to the studio. It was immediately easy to see why.

On the roof of that one-story edifice, there stood, his arms outstretched, the strange and fearful figure of a man. He faced the fire, and the flames threw streaks of flowing red against his dark face and his long white clothing. I had seen him somewhat so before, but that earlier fire was not to be compared with this; if I had thought of Jamshid in a general way as a big man, now he loomed huge—and with a presence beyond nature.

He was singing. Or call it a chant, if you will. As the sound of the fire lessened a little, the melody of Jamshid's song impaled the night on the sharp points of dismal quarter tones, while long, triumphant drawn-out vowels trembled between the Oriental consonants.

It was a prayer—that much I could make out when the words of his singing verged on Arabic. But of what he prayed and to what end, I would not know had my father not been handy—with his avid ear for language and his verbal memory. From him I have begged a translation of what Jamshid sang, and I give it here as he gave it to me.

> "Lord, the Light-bringer, Father of fire,
>   Thou who despisest the death of our bodies,
>   Take to thy light and purge with thy fire
>   The dead we offer, the dead we burn.
>   Lord of the lightning, Friend of fire,
>   Sun of our souls, consume our bodies;
>   Let the flesh perish—so that our spirits
>   Live with light and live with fire."

My father insists that the language suffers in translation and that his version is only approximate. He himself had never before heard the tongue that Jamshid spoke, but he claims that it resembled the Tadzhik dialect. However that may be, the power of the old prayer flowed through Jamshid like the current in a wire: we were ourselves electrified, incapable of motion.

Over and over, the high priest wove his spell. And as he sang, the fire inside the house died slowly down. The sparks no longer flew so furiously upward. Only a few flames rose above the furnace rim.

Jamshid was silent.

Chapter

28

Cars were beginning to arrive as we made our way back around the house. The pillar of fire by night had alerted a few wakeful souls, and curiosity had drawn them to the scene. Like a quaint anticlimax, a single fire engine appeared. I never learned where it had come from, but under Officer Peabody's direction, three sleepy-looking firemen ventured in by the front door. They reappeared almost at once, reporting that the inside rooms were very hot but that nothing they had seen was actually scorched. After some consultation together, they decided not to force the laboratory door until the fire in that room had had time to subside completely. A spectator who seemed to know Officer Peabody offered his own car to take Butrus to the hospital. The offer was accepted, and Charlie Vickers went along.

Just about then the pilgrims from the beach arrived, a weary-looking crew. Mr. Torquil seemed, I thought, the most done in, and Mrs. Little far and away the spriest. Chicken offered me the last of her ham sandwiches and expressed some disappointment at the fire's being nearly out.

"Don't tell the children, Posy, but I think Mrs. Budding set it—before she went for the police, I mean. She's a very peculiar woman in my book. Ever since her husband died, she's been looking for excitement."

I was unimpressed by this diagnosis but let her run on.

"I'll have a chance to watch her reaction," she said. "We've got it all settled: Lucy and Mrs. Budding are coming home with Grandma and me; you and your father and Warburton are to stay at Mr. Torquil's place—he's got plenty of room—until things settle down."

Lucy had joined us but too late, I hoped, to hear the comments on her mother.

"Just for tonight, we'll be visitors," she said. "And my goodness! The night's nearly gone."

So it had. The moon had set, and toward the east the night sky wore a lighter blue. Headlights along the drive began to have a pale and watery look. Lucy provided further information: "The firemen think that Sexton's Prim will be ready for fixing—you know, cleaning and all that—sometime tomorrow. I rather wish, Posy, that you'd be with Munce and me. You seem so able to cope, somehow."

I have never felt more flattered in my life.

Mr. Snow joined us. "Where's that there Jamshid?" he wanted to know. "He wasn't inside that part that burned, was he?"

I assured him that when last heard from, Jamshid was singing on a nearby roof. A moment later we were approached by the man himself, all signs of hieratic fervor vanished, once more the perfect servant. He addressed himself to me, and it was difficult to think of him in terms of priestly rapture.

"Excuse me, *âghâ*—if I may speak to you alone?"

"All right," I said. I viewed him with considerable reservation. We withdrew to the shelter of Mr. Peabody's Buick.

"I trust the *âghâ* now understands my position?"

"No," I said. "I don't believe I do."

He gave a sigh—the patient Orient confronted with the undiscerning West. "I am sorry for that. Time will **perhaps** explain. I have assigned myself the task of watching here. It is an agreeable thing to the policeman. And the *khanoûm*—Mrs. Budding—and the children will need someone. You will be staying on, *âghâ?*"

"I'm not sure," I said. "It depends on a lot of things."

"So it does," he agreed. "Meanwhile, may I ask the *âghâ* but one more question?"

"Go ahead," I told him.

"It is about the *tashrif*—the doctor Sarx. There is news of him? He escaped perhaps?"

"I think," I said, "that there is very little likelihood of our seeing him again."

Jamshid bowed his head. But whether it was in grief or satisfaction, I am unable to say.

Chapter

29

One month later to a day, my father and I were seated in the east lounge of the University Club. Refreshments were before us, and the cool air of the big room felt grateful after the summer street. We had just come from the Torquils' wedding at St. Thomas's; Mrs. Budding—I should say Mrs. Torquil— had looked young and lovely; the twins had behaved themselves most remarkably well.

It was the first time I had seen the Gnome since the climax of affairs at Sexton's Prim, and we had much to talk about. There were several questions that I wanted answered, and one or two points on which he himself needed information.

"You don't think, then, that you'll visit Chicken Little over Labor Day?" he asked.

"No," I said. "I don't believe so. After all, I've seen her nearly every day for three weeks. Frankness compels me to admit that between ham sandwiches and her grandmother's quotations—"

"Why!" he interrupted. "I thought you two were making serious plans together."

"No," I said. "To tell the truth, I'm waiting for Lucy."

He nodded gravely. "An extraordinary child," he agreed. "Mata Hari in a pinafore."

"Speaking of pinafores," I said, "where on earth did you get those shaggy knickerbockers that you wore at the Cape?"

He evaded my question. "They were nice and warm," he said, "especially in the casket."

"And how did you get into that?" I asked. "How, indeed, did you get into everything?"

"The whole thing started in a casket," said my father. "Not the one that I was in. Another one. A casket that didn't have anybody in it. That was the trouble."

"How?" I asked. "Should there have been?"

"There should. Let's see now. It was on June 3—June 3 or June 4—that the business began in Creepy Hollow."

"The Westchester cemetery?"

"Yes. A dip fault with a two-foot throw occurred in lots 43 and 44."

"How's that again?"

"There was a dislocation of the land—a slip of the earth—affecting the security of several graves. These things can happen, especially in graveyards that are old. The Creepy Hollow people have faced it before, and in this case they decided that the graves must be moved. The owners were discreetly advised—they could hardly object to a safety measure—and new concrete vaults were prepared in a space some distance from the fault—all this *on* the cemetery, of course. Unfortunately, in the process of moving the bodies, a crane hook slipped, and one of the caskets fell from some feet above ground into a new excavation. It didn't fall straight, and part of it hit the waiting concrete wall. The casket was cloth-covered wood—a common enough type—and the wood split end to end. If the casket had held ordinary human remains, it is doubtful whether the damage would have been so severe. As it was, however, the split was positively destructive. The broken casket had to be hauled up again, and—in the judgment of a director who was hurriedly called in—replaced. Since most people's families really prefer not to know about such things, replacement would be confidential and listed as a 'minor adjustment' in the cemetery records. But alas for discretion! When everything was ready for the 'adjustment' to take place, the superintendent in charge found in the broken casket not a human cadaver but an artificial figure carved out of light wood and covered with hieroglyphics.

"For some reason or other this superintendent fellow (who seems to have gotten his appointment through a modest skill at landscaping) assumed that he was himself responsible, or would be held so. In a purple sort of panic, he went ahead with the transfer, swearing his workmen to secrecy and only informing the cemetery office when his conscience smote him two weeks later. Greatly embarrassed by a second exhumation, the officials debated notification of the next of kin and after some delay decided that the police should be told first. This they did by informing a local resident who happened to be both a police department chieftain in New York and a director of the cemetery. This gentleman, for reasons best known to himself, put off a further report to the authorities, and it was not until the first week in July that the county ordered an official exhumation.

"The name plate on the broken casket, by the way, read 'Warren Budding'—with the dates, '1921-1962.' "

"Mrs. Budding's husband!" I exclaimed rather stupidly.

"And the twins' father. But the point is, he wasn't *in* the thing."

"He died, didn't he?"

"Of course he died. I'll get to that in a minute. I haven't told you yet how *I* got involved."

"Pray do," I said.

"It goes back to Jamshid," said my father. "Jamshid—as you know—was the Buddings' servant. Where they acquired him on their travels, I don't know—"

"In Tehran," I put in, "when Mr. B. was cultural attaché there. Lucy told me."

"I see," said my father. "Well, they got a good servant. Devoted to master and mistress and, in an unobtrusive way, to the children. The family knew, of course, that he was a Parsi. I doubt if they knew that he was a Parsi clergyman."

"A clergyman?"

"In a way. A strict religionist, at any rate. Which made it all the stranger for him to elect the service of an archaeologist— an Egyptologist especially."

"Why so?"

"Because of the Parsis' particular feeling about the dead. They never preserve bodies, you know. Either they go in for a kind of cremation or expose their dead on wooden towers and let vultures do the rest. Fire is more than useful: it's symbolic because it consumes, and it's terribly important for the human body to be consumed. Otherwise, the human spirit is imprisoned—and any sort of preservation is the worst imprisonment of all."

"But I don't quite see why Jamshid should have objected to Egyptology," I said.

"Because of the contact with mummies. But the point is, in Mr. Budding's case—we really shouldn't call him 'Mister'; he was positively gravid with degrees—but in Mr. Budding's case, Jamshid *didn't* object. To him, apparently, Mr. Budding was a liberator: by his digging he set spirits free. This was fine; this was all the best. Whereas, when he got to know Dr. Sarx, he found a man who was dedicated to what he most loathed—the confinement of living spirits in an earthly prison.

"Of course, the realization must have come slowly. After Warren Budding's illness, Jamshid consented readily enough to visit in the States during his master's convalescence. As far as he was concerned, Sarx was just another scholar with the same interests and purposes as Budding. Then gradually, he began to see some differences. He found out where Sarx made his money—at least in part from the preservation of the dead.

He overheard unpleasant conversation on the part of the two Egyptian assistants. Jamshid was poles away from them—in language, in intelligence, and, most important of all, in belief. But he found them *in situ* when he came and took them in his stride for a while as ignorant *fellahin*, beneath his notice.

"Then his master's health grew worse instead of better. He himself became increasingly suspicious of good Dr. Sarx. Very astutely, he deduced that Sarx was using Budding's knowledge—and the younger man was truly a great scholar—to promote his own evil projects.

"I have no doubt that certain Oriental instincts aided Jamshid in his conclusions. One must remember that the man was a mystic, a devoted follower of the great Zoroaster, a modern colleague of the Magi. To him, Sarx's notion of captive spirit was abomination. When he saw such theories threatening those he loved, there was no step he would not take.

"While his master lived, he had the run of the laboratory, and there he found ample evidence of Dr. Sarx's designs. While his master lived, he said nothing but watched like a hawk over those whom he considered his responsibility. When Budding died—"

"By fair means or foul?" I asked.

"It's too late to find out," my father said. "Putting the best face on it, let's suppose the children's father died of purely natural causes. Before he died, the archaeologist let Jamshid know that he wished to be cremated. But once he was dead, Sarx issued a family manifesto to the effect that his former colleague had requested burial—with the customary *pompes funèbres*. Mrs. B., it seems, was in no shape to protest; so—more or less over Jamshid's dead body—a private service was held at Sexton's Prim, and Mr. Budding's remains were shipped to his family plot at Creepy Hollow—in a sealed casket, of course."

"Only they weren't," I put in.

"Only they weren't. Right first time. But though Jamshid

182

suspected, he wasn't sure. And I think he might have been willing to accept mere Christian burial—or rationalized it somehow—if he hadn't suspected something far more hideous."

"Such as what?"

"Such as the doctor's keeping Budding's body in his lab to work on while a spurious casket was shipped to New York."

"Jamshid suspected this?"

"He did more. In the doctor's study, he came across some memoranda that were a total giveaway. Sarx was keeping a kind of journal in which, like many a lesser man, he applauded himself in advance: how marvelous it will be!—and how the world will wonder!—when I do thus and so. Jamshid read the journal, and he searched the lab. In one of the central drawers, he found the nearly finished mummy of a man about forty years old. The Parsi decided to act."

"You mean he decided to take care of Sarx?"

"In a way. At first, his idea seems to have been sabotage. Anything—anything to harass the processes of preservation! He came to regard the Egyptian assistants as mortal enemies. He even went so far as to waylay the hearse. Two or three times he ambushed Vickers from the roadside."

"I remember one occasion," I said.

"Then he decided to write to New York. He knew that his late master's burial address was Creepy Hollow, so that is where he wrote. I have a copy of the very letter here, for this is where *I* come in.

"He wrote," my father explained, "to Walter Quicken. He didn't know it, but he did."

"Walter Quicken?" The name rang a faint bell. "The submarine commander?"

"The former submarine commander, who happens now to be the mayor of Creepy Hollow. I'll read the letter to you. It's addressed 'To the Mayor, Creepy Hollow, New York.' A very fair European hand, has Jamshid.

" 'To the Mayor,
Creepy Hollow,
New York.

Serene Highness:

In the name of Fire and in the name
of Light: greetings. Let there be made at Your
Highness' leisure search of the case purporting to
contain the flesh and bones of Warren Budding
whose name the Sun called six days since. This case
is digged into your field of dead. By the Fire and
by the Light you are adjured to act on behalf of

Your expectant servant,
B. Jamshid'

"There follows a line of what I take to be Huzvaresh—it certainly isn't Tadzhik."

"Some style!" I murmured. "How'd you get the letter?"

"The night you left for the Cape—before I even knew that Australia was canceled—I had dinner at the Players. You know how empty it is down there on some summer evenings. Well, who should be in the bar but Walter Quicken? And what should Walter have in his burning pocket but this letter? He read it to me and asked whether I thought the thing was genuine, the work of a nut, or what. I said it sounded genuine enough, and then I caught a glimpse of the envelope. 'Sexton's Prim, West Orleans' was printed on the back flap. Since I'd just shipped you off to that very address, you can imagine my interest. Walter noticed my reaction right away: 'What does this mean to you?' he asked me. I explained briefly, and I well remember his reply. 'This very morning,' he said, "I was notified by the County Examiner that Warren Budding's grave contains a dummy instead of a corpse.' He couldn't have urged me in more clearly. It wasn't long after dinner that I started sending telegrams and making plans."

184

"Don't tell me you grew a beard that night," I protested.

"No, I admit that the beard was a bit of *décor appliqué.* It tickled horribly under the mummy's mask."

"And you decided right away to join me?"

"It sounded like fun—and possible excitement. I spent a morning boning up on Sarx—a man of his financial prominence isn't hard to get information on. I also found out through an indiscreet girl in his purchasing department that he had sample caskets sent to New England almost every week. She even told me proudly that a specimen was then on its way—'International Casket's latest demicouch,' she said. I caught up with it at the Hyannis freight station, and you know the rest."

"Excuse me, but I certainly do not. How on earth did you get into the thing? There must have been people around."

"At Hyannis? Certainly there were. I fused a double cherry bomb with a longish bit of string and left it in the men's room. Then I walked out to where the casket sat on a baggage truck. A porter was talking to his buddy, but when the bomb went off, they both dashed into the station. In the twinkling of an eye"—he spoke in mock-heroic vein—"Major Oregon Flower had hit the sack. Or rather, the 'demicouch.' Very comfortable it was, too, with 'genuwine' dacron upholstery— and my bottle of guaranteed oxygen. To be sure, I fiddled the latch so I could open the lid whenever I wanted to. Charlie Vickers would have been rather surprised if he'd looked around." He laughed again. "But it was good of you to help carry me in."

"And you slept down there that night—in the casket where we left it in the hall?"

"I might have—except for the traffic. You and Jamshid kept the place pretty busy. Poor Jamshid, you must have given him a frightful shock that night!"

"He reacted to it very quickly," I said. "And what was *he*

doing there anyway—particularly if he had such scruples about mummies and all?"

"He was trying to exorcise the evil wrought by Dr. Sarx. Didn't he light a fire? I thought so. And first, I suppose, he opened the drawer where Budding's mummy was."

"Was it actually in there?"

"It was indeed. Poor Jamshid was trying by his native arts to undo the doctor's doing—to 'lead captivity captive,' so to speak. You were a total surprise, and after he discovered who you were, he didn't know what to do with you. You were a newcomer and an unknown quantity: he didn't have you labeled—which was just the effect that Dr. Sarx wanted when he advertised for an extra inmate to confuse the madhouse."

"You mean that all along, I was—er—dust in their eyes?"

"My boy, you were a bright red herring. Old Jamshid had to think about you—needed some time to make up his mind. His silly prank along the road the night that you arrived—his firing on the hearse, I mean—was partly the culmination of a scare campaign against Charlie (and Charlie had a shrewd idea who was shooting at him) and partly an attempt to frighten you."

"Was he out of his head?" I asked.

"No, I don't think so. But he certainly was mixed up. I don't really believe he'd have wanted to harm Charlie. I notice you say that he shot at your tires. It was simply that he had to *do* something, make a gesture, vindicate his own standpoint. I suppose we could say that he was torn between compulsion and taboo. Compulsion forced him into the laboratory for his rites. Taboo kept him away from Sarx's equipment. When you caught him—or he caught *you*—that night, he was on foreign soil. Surrounded by what he called the 'things of death,' he couldn't think—couldn't make up his mind about you, for instance. So after he'd knocked you out, he tied you to that mortician's preparation table and went his way. And there you were—till I let you loose and pinned a few words of advice on your back. Eventually, he returned to the lab, you know, and was mystified to find you gone. He reassured himself by supposing that you hadn't recognized him."

"I broke that dream up the next morning," I said.

"I know you did. And the two of you wound up by trying to bluff each other. It was fun to watch."

My father pulled out his pipe. "Snow sent me this the other day—very kind of him. I'd left it down in his shanty. I thought perhaps you'd recognize it."

"I almost did," I said, remembering the trip with Lucy to the beach.

"I saw you on the shore," my father told me. "Twice, in fact —morning and afternoon. I had checked in with Torquil— an old OSS-er, you know. That was when I gave the note to Mrs. Little—she's a grand old girl."

"But you didn't know *her* before, did you?" I asked.

"No. Simply told her I was your father. There's no recommendation like it. Plus name and rank, of course. I knew she was a love the minute I set eyes on her. Besides, I was getting really anxious about the children. Those Egyptians were so clumsy."

"The Egyptians! Were Butrus and Ali trying to kill the children?"

"Not kill, I think. Maim, incapacitate, immobilize, I think. That's why they scored so many near misses. Sarx had some sort of idea that the twins must be grounded, readily available for an immediate experiment and incapable of normal evasion. His reading of the decans—the stars to you and me— had him all on edge. Proceedings might have to start at any minute. That's why I went to such lengths about Warburton.

"But he gave his *fellahin* the shoddiest of orders, and they themselves had small imaginations. The fact made them doubly dangerous. Ali's ploy with the brace in the dory was pathetic, of course; but if it didn't do anything else, it alibied

187

Sarx. As a matter of fact, you remember, Sarx stayed carefully out of the picture that whole night."

"But he knew what they were doing? No wonder he wasn't surprised about the truck!"

"He wasn't surprised at all. Butrus had probably let him down before."

An association formed, most belatedly, in my mind.

"Butrus!" I exclaimed. "I ought to have known it was Butrus in the garage because I recognized his footprint—the golf shoe with the pug marks. It was there on the floor of the barn, and then I forgot it—even when I saw it again after he'd been slugged! But—but if it was Butrus who was carrying out orders, who knocked *him* on the head?"

"I'm afraid it was Jamshid," my father admitted.

"Jamshid?" It didn't seem to fit. "But why?"

"Jamshid no longer had a key to the lab. He knew that Butrus had one, and he knew only one way of getting it. He was preparing, you see, for his night's invasion of the inner sanctum. He had no idea how he confused the issue for you."

"And his tale about the village feud was all—"

"Poppycock—a delightful word. Did you know that poppycock came from the colloquial Danish 'pappekak'—which means soft dung? Interesting, isn't it?"

I agreed. You have to.

"The second garage incident was my fault," my father went on. "I didn't realize he was there in the loft—Ali, that is. I knew Lucy was with you, and I had told you to stick with her. When Ali let loose with that chair, I could have wept—at the sheer carelessness of it. No criticism of you, of course, but I was glad I had arranged for the boy's total disappearance."

"Yes," I said. "Yes." I was sure he was trying to be difficult. "Do you mind letting me in on that disappearance business? What or who were the actual abductors?"

"My dear boy, surely you recognized your father's voice on

the telephone—as readily as I recognized that of Mr. Green-sleeves?"

"That was you on the phone?"

"None other. I wanted you worried, you see—about the whole kidnapping business. Then you would worry Uncle Cutty, and Uncle Cutty would stay away from the police—even if it cost him money—and he would take the first possible opportunity of getting the Buddings together and putting on his Main Attraction—before some essential participant turned up missing.

"With Mr. Snow's help, I got hold of Warburton in the morning. That very wise young man had decided it was time to disappear—at least temporarily—for as long as he could be sure that someone was looking after Lucy. I assured him that, between us, you and I would do just that, and he agreed to the kidnapping caper. As a matter of fact, he fixed the price of the ransom."

"And I suppose he was sitting beside your phone when you and I had our conversation."

"No. He was safely installed at the Littles'—Chicken and Grandma both relished the scheme—and I was calling from the phone at the gate. As soon as you answered, I knew Sarx must be out and assumed he had gone to the bank. I suppose I might be held for extortion, but not, I feel, for kidnapping. I was simply abetting Warburton's own decision. He said he enjoyed playing chess with Torquil."

"But Torquil was out with—the lady who is now his wife."

"Filling her in, you may be sure, on the subject of my general reliability."

"Then that's why she didn't ask about Warburton."

"I imagine so. In any case, I told Torquil to take his time, for with Mrs. B. and Uncle Cutty both out of the way, I had a pretty free run of the house. When I got there, you and Lucy had both disappeared, but I found you at the beach."

189

"You were down there that afternoon, too?"

"Just long enough to let Ali get into the garage loft—which he did by opening the floor in your bedroom. He must have had a hunch you'd stop in that old barn on your way back. I went to Sarx's study because I was sure you'd phone from there. But Ali and Butrus came in before you did, and Sarx was with them. I was behind the window curtains. After what seemed a long, long time—"

"Lucy and I were having tea," I explained.

"After a long time you came in, and they bagged you. Sarx led them out, and I stayed by the window so I could see if they took you away by car. When they didn't appear, I concluded you'd been stowed somewhere in the house. Almost at once, the squawk box began to talk."

"Meanwhile," I said, "Sarx or one of them had nabbed Lucy."

"Yes." He nodded. "That must have been the time. I didn't know about it, though—and besides, I could hear them talking to you over the bug in your room. Oh yes, I told you that. Well, everything you said up there—in this case, everything that Sarx said—came over a small loudspeaker in the study. I heard his genial banter—and at least I had you located.

"In a little while they came downstairs again. I nipped out of the study window just in time to miss the doctor. I wanted to find Lucy."

"—who, in the meanwhile," I suggested, "had been moved in next to me."

"Yes, but I didn't know it. All I knew was that she had disappeared. I didn't think of her own room for a long time—not till after I had let you loose. And then, of course, I had to get mixed up in the moving business. While they were all at the studio, I got Charlie to help me out with the extra casket. Only it wasn't exactly extra."

"How do you mean?"

"The late Mr. Budding was in it. I'd put him there myself

while you were having lunch. I had to show him to Charlie, but the mummy was good enough to convince him. We used the truck. Charlie had an errand in Hyannis, anyway. I fancy the folk at Creepy Hollow were glad to have their missing boy come home.

"Then I made some arrangements in the lab, which had been left unlocked for the movers. En route, I swiped a pair of overalls and reported to the studio for manual toil. Incidentally, those fellows from the village were careless: when they left, they forgot to relock the lab door."

"And I slept through all of that?"

"You certainly sounded like it when I came through your window."

A club servant replenished our drinks.

"After you left, I stopped at Lucy's room and switched her to yours. I didn't think they'd look there, and I knew that she could always use the ladder."

"She never noticed it," I said.

"If so," my father answered, "it's the first thing in her life she ever missed." He took a sip of his drink. "Most of the rest," he said, "you know."

"Did Jamshid set the fire?" I asked.

My father took some time before he answered. "It's hard to say. Fireproof as it seemed—and as its walls and flooring actually proved to be—that lab was cram-jam full of combustibles. When you work with mummies, you're dealing in natron, gum, gauze, cotton, unguents, and—in this case—modern preservatives. You wouldn't have to look very far for the makings. And there was that remark of Chicken Little's—remember? Something about Jamshid's being 'awfully busy with those rags and things.' I don't know. Of course, the man had motive enough—according to his own lights. To him, Sarx was an 'embalmer of Anubis,' an overseer of the hated Egyptian mysteries. In Jamshid's mind, the one escape possible for his master, Warren Budding, was the funerary pyre—

cremation. It was over a cremation that we saw him presiding; his prayer that night was a prayer of triumph.

"And the inside of that room was a regular ghat, you know. Afterwards, they said the walls and chests were simply twisted metal."

"But Jamshid's master wasn't there! You had—"

"Ah," said my father, "but Jamshid didn't know that." He looked out the window at the passers-by on Fifth Avenue. "As far as I'm concerned, he never will."

I felt the same way. "Tell me another thing," I said. "Whatever became of the ransom money? Or wasn't it real?"

"Oh, the money was real enough." My father gave me a long look. "As for what became of it, I don't believe I can answer that question." He paused. "I did hear, though, that Mr. Snow paid off his obligation on that land a week or so ago."

We were silent. The sound of water in Gannet Bay was something past and gone—the roaring of the laboratory fire, a fading memory.

"I suppose," I said, "that there's no doubt about the end of Dr. Sarx?"

My father did not answer. He was standing at the club-room window, staring intently north toward Fifty-fifth Street. Then: "If I'm not mistaken," he said, "Dr. Sarx is going into the St. Regis through the jewelry shop."

We looked at each other. With no further word, we hastened to the cloakroom desk and asked for our hats.